"Dr. Ross captures the human drama of living with serious chronic illness in 'The Perfect Match'. You will feel the real drama and emotion of what people with kidney failure must deal with when facing the need for life saving therapies like dialysis as well as the extraordinary gift of life that a kidney transplant represents."

Frank Maddux M.D.
Global Medical Director
Fresenius Medical Care

"In The Perfect Match, Dr. Ross is able to capture the trauma that families go through in donating a loved ones kidneys, the life-changing effects of starting dialysis, and the desperation many have in trying to get a kidney transplant in a medical thriller with many twists and turns. This book is an easy read, and hard to put down once you start reading it. I greatly enjoyed this cleverly written story."

Rick J. Barnett
President & Chief Executive Officer
Satellite Healthcare

The Perfect Match welcomes readers into a fascinating world that few get to visit. Good story-telling and evocative characters bring texture to underlying themes that touch on medical ethics and clinical decision-making. Wrapped up in a package of good old-fashioned drama, The Perfect Match provides insight into the patients' journey through healthcare and the path those with chronic diseases must navigate between hope and realism.

Leslie Trigg
Chief Executive Officer
Outset Medical

In The Perfect Match, Dr. Ross has created a medical thriller that compels the reader to continue to the end, while giving incredible insight about the life changing aspects of patients with kidney failure, kidney donation and and kidney transplantation. I was intrigued to realize the real life drama these people face and also fascinated by what I learned from reading The Perfect Match, as well as being highly entertained. I was unable to put it down once I started reading it!

Tina Eddy
Regional Vice President
Fresenius Kidney Care

As a kidney transplant recipient, I found that this heartfelt novel truly captures the trials and tribulations renal failure patients endure. Finding "The Perfect Match" is the ultimate life saving goal for every patient with chronic kidney disease.

Patricia Thompson

THE
PERFECT
MATCH

DENNIS ROSS

ARCHWAY
PUBLISHING

Archway Publishing books may be ordered
through booksellers or by contacting:

Archway Publishing
1663 Liberty Drive
Bloomington, IN 47403
www.archwaypublishing.com
1 (888) 242-5904

ISBN: 978-1-4808-7752-8 (sc)
ISBN: 978-1-4808-7750-4 (hc)
ISBN: 978-1-4808-7751-1 (e)

Library of Congress Control Number: 2019906767

Print information available on the last page.

Archway Publishing rev. date: 6/26/2019

I would like to thank my wife, Ann, for always supporting me. Her advice and suggestions in *The Perfect Match* were invaluable. I would also like to thank Tina Eddy, Jan Schmidt, Marya McCrae, Laura Roddy, and Dr. Lisa Weber for their help in editing the book and their encouragement in writing this story. Finally, I want to acknowledge the many patients that I have cared for over my career and thank them for letting me be part of their lives.

PROLOGUE

The young doctor, in his ill-fitting tuxedo, gasped when he saw Rosa Seratino sashay down the aisle toward the center stage wearing her fiery red, sequined gown. "Who the hell is that?" he whispered to the young man standing next to him, a man who was equally mesmerized.

"Come on—surely you know her," his friend whispered. "That's Rosa Seratino, and she's quite the opera sensation. Chicago Lyric Opera. The Met. She's the real thing."

"Why is she at a hospital fundraiser?" the young doctor asked. "Is she here alone? God, she's gorgeous. I think it's time she met a doctor." With boyish eagerness he brought her a glass of champagne, only to have her dismissively take a small sip and walk away.

The smitten doctor couldn't tear his eyes from Rosa as she mounted the stage and introduced herself. "I'd like to thank you for having me here this evening. We all know what an outstanding job Deaconess Hospital has done caring for our citizens' medical problems, and I'm honored to be part of this event. I'd like to start the evening by singing 'Casta Diva,' the ultimate soprano aria, from the opera

1

Norma by Bellini. It was sung best by Montserrat Caballé, so I hope I can give you a taste of how she would have sung this gorgeous piece."

As she sang, the young doctor felt himself swaying in seductive rhythm to the music, charmed like a cobra by a charmer's pungi. The crowd erupted, clapping enthusiastically and yelling out praise, but he led shouts of "brava" and "bravisima" above the applause while he pushed himself through the crowd to get closer to the stage and to her. But the doctor could also see the glowing eyes of the Chicago elite, pressing forward across the red carpeting of the crystal-chandeliered ballroom with tapestry-covered walls, trying to get closer to the performer, hoping to be recognized among the wealthy attendees.

Rosa gave a sweeping bow, leading into singing a second number as small beads of perspiration appeared on her forehead. Belting out "The Love Music" from Wagner's *Tristan und Isolde,* she swayed her hips.

The doctor could only imagine he was the recipient of her seductive, graceful movements. He pushed even closer in the crowded room. At the end of the aria, he clapped until his palms were red. He didn't want to miss this opportunity to be the first to congratulate her as she stepped off the platform.

He offered his hand, saying, "I feel like I'm Don Jose, being swept away by Carmen. You've smitten me with your voice. I've never heard anything like it."

"I'm glad you enjoyed it, Doctor. It's refreshing to see at least someone knows something about opera in this crowd."

"You remind me of Maria Callas—but of course you're even lovelier than she."

"You're skilled at the art of flattery, Doctor, and as you must know, we opera singers love compliments. But enough talk. My feet are killing me, and I need another drink."

"I can help you on both counts," he replied. "Follow me to the hallway so I can take a look at your feet."

Rosa eased herself into an overstuffed chair just outside the ballroom entrance and slipped off her shoes.

"Wow, there's a mammoth blister on your left heel. This is obviously the problem. I wouldn't be able to put one foot in front of the other if I had a blister like this. I guess women just get used to putting their feet in these amazingly skinny shoes. I've got some bandages in my room, and I can tape this up for you. Why don't you just take your shoes off and follow me."

The key turned easily in the lock of his tenth-floor suite.

"Would you like some bourbon? It's a great painkiller," he said. "You'll have to take off those stockings for me to dress this heel properly. I'll go get some ointment."

When he returned, her face became twisted as she drank the bourbon straight. He lifted her gown and slowly rolled the silk stockings down her leg. He reached the area of her foot where the blister was located. But he found he couldn't take his hands off her leg or resist going inappropriately higher. His desire for her grew. Much to his surprise, as their eyes met, he could see Rosa express the same craving for him and didn't resist.

Looking up at her, he sensed she'd done this before.

"I'm lonely—understand?"

"Well, that's the third thing I can help you with, Rosa. I'm divorced, and I know how it feels to be lonely." He rose from his kneeling position. Beads of perspiration trickled down his forehead, as the passion of the moment was insurmountable.

"I don't think you should be walking at all," he said as he deftly carried her into his bedroom.

The next half hour passed quickly. Rosa abruptly got out of bed and got dressed.

"What's the matter? Did I do something wrong? Spend the night with me!"

"Are you crazy? I'm married, and I just wasn't thinking clearly."

"Are you afraid of your husband?"

"No, but you should be."

He paused, concerned by the comment. "Well, can I call you sometime?"

"Look, I don't know your name—and I don't want to know your name. This never occurred. Understand? Never happened. If you know what's best for you—best for both of us—never call me."

As Rosa left the room, he thought, *I should have used a condom; what was I thinking? It was only once, and I doubt she has anything I could catch. What did I get myself into. Smiling, it was pretty good actually.*

He reached the lobby, and his friend cried out, "Where have you been?"

"Oh, just treating a patient."

◖◗

Henry Unser, a bald, plump little man with an apron around his waist, saw Tillie Winslow enter his grocery store, Central Supermarket, located in south Chicago's middle-class neighborhood. It wasn't a big supermarket but a mom-and-pop store that this area of town loved. Giving that personal touch was what everyone liked about this family-owned business.

"Are you Mrs. Winslow?"

Henry knew she loved this attention, and these little old ladies would often fawn over him if he spent time complimenting them. Her round face beamed as he took notice of her.

"Your friend Gretchen Knicks told me you make the best pies. Is that true?"

Blushing, Tillie responded, "I do have people tell me my pies are the best."

"Then you're in for a treat today. We have just received new peaches that are out of this world. They're so juicy that I think they would make a fantastic peach pie. Let me show you where they are." He led her to the produce department.

After helping Mrs. Winslow, Henry put his arm around Tom Tatman, the produce manager, and walked him to the back of the store.

"Damn good peaches. Keep up the good work. By the way, did you see the paper today?" he asked, handing the business section to Tom. "Those bastards at Centco. They're doubling their size to add a discount grocery. Just another chain that's trying to put us out of business. Well, by God, they're not going to do it."

Henry thought, *How can I survive in this environment? My store is small compared to the giant chains.* He had limited inventory and couldn't provide a lot of the foods found in these giant grocers.

I just don't want to sell out to anyone. I love owning this place. It's the only thing I know to do. Pondering this, he wandered into his office since it was finally closing time and found his way back to his office to study the books.

Maybe I can find some new suppliers to lower my costs so I can be more competitive. I know that my customers like me, but price can be everything.

The store was dim with the exception of the bright light in the office where Henry worked. Focused on the numbers, he didn't hear the man walk to the back of the store and appear in his office.

Startled, he looked up. "Who are you?"

"Sammy. Sammy Berino."

"How'd you get in here? The store's closed."

"They must have left the back door open."

"So what do you want?"

"I'm here to ask ya if you've decided about the offer my client has made for your store."

"What offer?"

"The offer Mr. Seratino made. Two million, five hundred thousand dollars. We think this is very generous."

"Oh, that. Sorry, not interested."

Sammy moved to Henry's side, set down his briefcase, removed the offer, and handed it over. "Mr. Seratino is prepared to increase that offer to three million."

"Look, you don't seem to understand. I have no interest in selling my store. This is my baby. It's not a money thing."

"I know Mr. Seratino will be very disappointed." Sammy replaced the offer inside the briefcase. Then, reaching inside, he removed a revolver with a silencer.

In the next instant, the only thing that Henry Unser saw was the barrel of the gun pointed at his head. Before he could react, a bright light appeared, followed by total darkness as blood and brains splattered on the opposing wall. His face struck the desk as he fell.

"Too bad. It was a good deal."

CHAPTER 1

Eighteen years later

Mickey Ward enjoyed the rumble of his powerful Harley as it squealed out of the parking lot of Mulligan's Tavern. *Missy can go to hell. Someday she'll regret having ignored me, because I'll have moved on.* The cold wind whipped his long blond hair into his face, but the four beers he had just downed gave him a sense of warmth in spite of the frigid air.

He instinctively headed toward his favorite path for one last ride before the December snows set in. He knew the path well. It was his imaginary racetrack, complete with obstacles and jumping ramps—even though the true obstacles were the debris, wooden barricades, wire fencing, and No Trespassing signs. He skillfully directed his bike to avoid the potholes and broken boards. Winters were brutal in Chicago, and Mickey knew his life was about to change. He had gotten a job now and was going to start at the Auto Parts Unlimited just before the Christmas holiday.

He twisted the throttle, and his Harley lurched forward at

a faster pace. As Mickey approached Ninth and Clements, he accelerated, trying to catch a yellow light before it turned red. Staring ahead, he caught a glimpse of a police car with lights flashing and sirens blaring and it appeared to race toward the same intersection. Mickey gasped as he realized there was no way to avoid a collision with a speeding Monte Carlo—without its lights on—that was being pursued by the police.

As Mickey slammed on the brakes, the motorcycle tires screeched, the Harley fishtailing frantically toward its inevitable doom. The explosion of tire and metal of Mickey's motorcycle striking the front fender of the car was the last sound Mickey heard, ever.

⟨⟩

The explosion could be heard several blocks away, echoing through the corridors of the abandoned warehouse alleys. The remains of the shattered motorcycle were strewn across the adjacent parking lot, taking their place among the other pieces of scrap metal left to rust and decay from a bygone era. The young rider was catapulted over the hood of the car and landed on the pavement opposite the collision. His mangled body lay twisted among the other items of debris found in the deserted parking lot. The Monte Carlo veered to the right after the force of the impact.

"Did you see that?" Officer Joe Blandchard asked his partner, Mike Freeman. "A body flew over the hood. I'm heading over."

"Sorry, Joe, can't help you. I got these guys rounded up. Just cuffing them now."

The scene was not well lit, but Joe Blandchard could easily tell from the light of his flashlight that the young man lying in a rapidly growing pool of blood was in grim condition.

Blood poured from a large gash in the victim's head, and his leg was in a distorted position suggesting multiple fractures of the femur. He felt a wave of nausea come over him, but he regained his senses quickly enough to call over his walkie-talkie for an ambulance.

"Mike, get over here!" he screamed. Joe moved closer to the ashen body and observed that the crumpled form was still breathing. He knelt beside the man and felt for a pulse, which was rapid and thready.

"I'm Officer Blandchard, and help is on the way," he said to the limp body lying in a pool of blood, not believing this injured person heard anything. "Mike! You coming with that first aid kit?"

"Sorry it took me so long, but that group of kids took a lot of handling before I could get them under control. I knew you'd be busy over here. Man! It was a struggle. One guy was starting to run, but I grabbed him just as he was makin' his break. But you don't need to worry, they're all caught and I've got 'em under control. Backup should be here in a minute too. George answered, and I said—"

"Tell me this later. I can't believe this guy's about to code and you ramble on about catching those guys. We've got a major injury here, you understand?"

"Sorry, Joe. Wasn't thinkin'. Here's the kit. How can I help?"

"Grab that big bandage. We've got to try and stop this bleeding if we can. Where the hell is that ambulance? I told them Ninth and Clements. What's taking so long?"

In the distance the ambulance's siren wailed its imminent arrival. Mike Freeman ran to the intersection and flailed his arms in the air to alert the EMS crew to the exact location of the victim.

"Hey, guys, over here," Blandchard yelled to the

paramedics. "This guy's a mess. Blood everywhere, not a great pulse, won't respond to me.

The paramedics grabbed a stretcher, defibrillator, and a kit for intravenous fluids and took charge of the critical medical situation because they knew they had little time to spare if they were to save this man.

"Boy, you guys are good. Got that IV in right away. I couldn't get much of pulse, so hopefully those fluids that you started will help."

"Let's get rolling! This guy's got a serious head injury, and we have only minutes if we hope to have him survive. Deaconess is probably the closest trauma center, so let's head there," the chief paramedic said. "I've radioed ahead to the emergency room, and they know we're en route. They'll be ready for us."

Blandchard picked up a billfold that had fallen out of the bag Mickey had attached to his motorcycle.

"Hmmm. Where is that damn name?" Using his flashlight, he found the driver's license. "Ward, Mickey Ward."

CHAPTER 2

Gerhart Siller felt good this morning driving his new sleek Jaguar to work. Maneuvering around the corner at University Place and driving into the garage, he accelerated and loved the feel, the responsiveness of his car. Sleek. Powerful. Fast. But as the car reached the second level, the motor screeched with an unusual grinding sound of metal against metal.

Strange, Gerhardt Siller thought. *This is a new car.* Again he tried to accelerate, but this time the Jaguar began to lose power as it approached the next level, and the cat-like sound under the hood became even more intense. But then the car seemed to regain strength and move forward. On the next level, as he neared his parking spot at the Providence University administrative building, the car began to slow again and this time died for good.

What's wrong? he thought, noting that it was 7:21 a.m. and that he was at least six minutes behind schedule. Trying in vain to restart his new Jaguar, a large-hatted man with an acne-scarred face and in a trench coat approached his car.

"Need help, Mr. Siller?" the man asked.

"Damn car. Killed twice this morning. Wait, how do you know my name?"

"My client has been waiting for you to call him. He never heard back."

"And who's your client? I don't remember anyone whom I haven't called."

"Emilio Seratino. He has agreed to make a donation to your institution, but in return he wants his boy to attend your school."

"Look, I don't handle donations to the university, and I don't deal with admissions. And quite frankly, I don't know your client."

"Don't tell me you can't control who gets in."

"You need to call the admissions office and the foundation office. They could help you."

"My boss thinks you can help us. After all, you're the head honcho, right?"

"I can't do much. Besides, I need to deal with my car now."

"I think that you should remember to put oil in the car."

"But I just had the oil changed yesterday. I've driven the car only ten thousand miles, so that shouldn't be a problem."

"Siller, the motor is ruined. Don't worry. The company that changed your oil will replace the motor. You can claim they didn't tighten the drain plug. But I would think seriously about helping Mr. Seratino. He doesn't like to be ignored."

The large man turned and walked away, leaving Siller sitting in his car wondering what to make of all this.

Seeing the security guard, he called out, "Hey, Charlie, I need a hand."

"Sure, Mr. Siller. What's the problem?"

"My car died. I think the motor just blew up. It may be out of oil."

"Boy, that's too bad. Beautiful car. Let me help you push it into a parking spot."

Gerhardt Siller rushed to the administrative building and wiped the beads of sweat from his forehead. Taking the elevator to the tenth floor, he hurried into his office where the palatial space was elegantly appointed. His secretary's desk was positioned just outside to control foot traffic. Betty, his secretary, stood up immediately as Siller rushed in.

"Running a little late, sir?" Betty asked gently.

Irritated by the comment, he didn't answer. "Betty, is everything all set?"

"Yes, sir, it's all on your desk," she said politely.

The massive space for the president had a large oval rosewood desk and a high-backed, black leather chair. Lying on the desk were neatly arranged papers for today's meeting. A large bookcase stood in one corner of the room and contained leather-bound classic novels and a handful of journals. There were two soft chairs to accommodate guests.

Siller glanced at the small bar that stood in one corner of the room. *Too early for scotch!*

Siller loathed anyone's use of car trouble as an excuse to be late to a meeting, so he ignored Betty's comment and rushed into the beautifully appointed conference room after grabbing the documents. He checked his watch—7:29 a.m.

Ha! I'm not late after all, he thought. *Hell of a morning.*

"Good morning, gentlemen. Thank you for your promptness. Let us begin by hearing a review of the financial status of the university by our comptroller, Mr. Hancock."

None of the attendees would have dreamed of being late. Gerhart Siller had been known to lock the meeting room doors once sessions began. Others had been reprimanded or dismissed for arriving a mere five minutes late.

Siller's mind wandered as he thought about his Jaguar.

Who would want to destroy my car? Siller nodded responses to the ongoing discussion, but his real thoughts were elsewhere. Surprisingly, there was agreement among the attendees this year, and a modest tuition increase passed with ease. The meeting concluded with handshakes and smiles, and no one seemed to notice that Siller was upset.

As Siller left the room, he turned the matter over in his mind. *Who could have been so angry with me?* He instructed Betty to call in an excuse to Deaconess Hospital so he would not have to attend tonight's board meeting. He then noticed his phone blinking, indicating he had a message. Pressing play, he heard a familiar voice.

"Mr. Siller, I spoke to you about your car in the parking lot today. I think you need some insurance. You know, insurance that no more accidents happen to you, like car motors exploding. Who knows? Maybe it will be the vacation home in Maine next. I would suggest you call the admissions office today so the insurance can go into effect. Oh, and by the way, the boy's name is Nickolas—Nick Seratino."

Siller hung up the phone and sank back in his chair. Thoughtful for a few moments, he pressed the intercom button. "Betty, get me the admission office."

CHAPTER 3

Mickey arrived at the emergency room with a blood pressure of 80/60 mm/Hg and a pulse of 120. The EMS technicians had intubated him en route and were ventilating him by hand to keep him alive.

Dr. Mike Floyd, the fifth-year surgical resident, was waiting in the emergency room with Dr. Tom Benton, a second-year resident, as his assistant.

Floyd completed his initial exam, ordered X-rays and blood tests, and called out, "I need a long spinal needle. We've got to check his abdomen for blood."

Inserting the needle into the abdomen he withdrew bright-red blood. "We've got ruptured organs—I'm guessing spleen. We've got to get this guy to surgery."

"Doctor, you need to see these X-rays that just posted on the computer. Radiology just called," the emergency room nurse said with some urgency.

"Pelvic fracture, femoral fracture, brain swelling on the CT scan. This guy is a train wreck!"

"I thought this was a motorcycle accident," a bewildered new graduate nurse replied.

Dr. Floyd scowled at her in disbelief, questioning whether or not she was kidding. "Where do they get these nurses?" he muttered as he turned to his assistant. "Tom, I'll call the neurosurgeon, and you page an orthopedist. We're going to need burr holes and intracerebral monitoring right away, and then we'll do the exploratory abdominal surgery. After that, we'll turn things over to the orthopedist, providing the patient's still alive by then. Tom, you contact Dr. Simpson, the on-call neurosurgeon, and I'll reach someone in orthopedics."

"We don't have a lot of time here, people," Floyd yelled. "Let's get this guy to surgery."

Leona Ward's simple two-bedroom apartment was dark when the phone rang. She sleepily imagined the ring to be part of a dream until she heard the voice of the police officer when she answered the phone.

"Hello, ma'am. Is this Mrs. Ward?"

"Yeah ... who's calling?"

"This is Officer Joe Blanchard of the Chicago Police Department. I'm calling in regard to a Mr. Mickey Ward. Do you know a Mr. Ward, ma'am?"

"Of course I know Mickey. He's my son. What about him? Is he in trouble? Heavens, it's 2:30 in the morning, and I thought he was home by now. Who is this again?"

"This is Officer Joe Blanchard of the Chicago Police Department. Your son, Mickey, was involved in a motorcycle accident a few hours ago. He has been taken to Deaconess Hospital."

"What for? Is he all right?"

"Well, his motorcycle hit a car at Ninth and Clements. A car ran a stop sign, and Mickey couldn't avoid the collision.

We believe he's badly hurt. He was in a coma when he was taken to the hospital. The doctor would have to tell you how he's doing; I'm only letting you know where he is. It's my understanding he is going into surgery now."

"Can I talk to him first? What did you say happened?"

"The accident occurred down at Ninth and Clements in the old warehouse district. Looks like a car and Mickey's motorcycle arrived at the intersection at about the same time and that Mickey probably tried to stop but couldn't. Your son was thrown over the hood of the car and landed on the pavement. He has a pretty bad head injury; he wasn't wearing a helmet."

"I think it best if you come to the hospital as soon as you can. Do you have someone who can take you?"

She realized this wasn't a dream. "I think I can drive myself," she answered weakly. "Let's see, Deaconess is at Twelfth and Pine, right?"

"Right. Is there anything I can do for you, Mrs. Ward?"

"I don't know what to ask for. I'm just so upset by all this. But I can get to the hospital myself. Just give me a second. I'll be right there."

Dressing quickly, she exited her home through the garage. Her '83 Cutlass rambled through the deserted neighborhood toward Deaconess emergency room.

Rushing toward the hospital entry, she passed ambulances and police cars along the way.

Approaching the receptionist, she said frantically, "I need to know about my son, Mickey Ward."

The receptionist nonchalantly looked up from her small cluttered desk, set down her nail file, and smiled at Leona. "Oh, yes. Mickey Ward arrived here about an hour or two ago and was declared a trauma I. They've taken him to surgery already, I believe. I can get the nurse who was in charge of that case if you give me a few minutes. I'm sure she'll be happy to talk to you."

Leona paced back and forth in the emergency room waiting area for what seemed an eternity. *What is going on in this place? Why can't they tell me anything? Where is that nurse they promised? What was he doing driving his motorcycle in December? It's cold, and who knows what could be going on at that time of night? That kid just never learns, but he's a good kid. I just pray he'll be okay. He may do stupid things at times, but he's a good kid. He just has to live through this.*

Fifteen minutes later, the charge nurse came through the swinging doors and found Leona, her face weary and eyes red from crying.

"Mrs. Ward? I'm Cindy Black, the charge nurse who helped when Mickey first came in. I think you know Mickey's in surgery and Dr. Floyd's operating on him right now. He'll be out to talk to you when he's finished. Your son has many injuries: fractured leg, fractured pelvis, and head injury with brain swelling, but we're doing the best we can for him. You can wait for him upstairs in the surgical waiting area if you like. I can take you there. I've called a chaplain to be with you, and he should be here any moment. I'll let Dr. Floyd know where you'll be, and he'll speak to you as soon as he's finished operating."

"Go find out what's going on! I've just got to know that he's okay! Is he alert?" Leona asked in exasperation.

"He's still in surgery. With a severe head injury, a badly broken leg, and internal injuries, there's a lot to deal with. We don't yet know the extent of any other injuries. Do you have an insurance card?"

"Yeah, I hope I can find it. It's one of those issued by the state. Is that all you can think about at this time? Well, I think Mickey's covered. He doesn't have a job right now, and he lives with me," Leona replied as she rummaged through the items in her heavily worn black handbag.

The nurse snatched the card as soon as Leona found it and whisked it off to the business office after escorting her to the surgery waiting room.

Leona reluctantly took a seat in the corner of the room near a heater and tried to stop shaking. No one else was there, but within minutes a young chaplain found her.

"Mrs. Ward? Is that correct?"

"Yes, yes ... I'm Leona Ward. Just call me Leona."

"Your son was injured in that awful accident, right?"

"Yes, he was in a motorcycle accident. Have you heard anything more about how he's doing? I can't seem to get much information around this place."

He shook his head. "I'm sorry. I don't have any news. Would you like me to pray with you?"

"I've already done that," Leona replied, annoyed at the seemingly endless delays.

"Mickey's a good kid," she began. "He should have worn a helmet, but he didn't. I know. He never listens to me about that. He has a good heart, though. He's stubborn—and man, he loves those tattoos. I tried to tell him not to waste his money, but you know how kids are."

The chaplain offered her the coffee in the pot left over from the previous shift. The Styrofoam cup of hot coffee warmed her cold hands, but the stale contents tasted bitter. Abandoned coffee cups lined the small end table, showing that other visitors had reached similar conclusions.

"Coffee's not that great," the chaplain said apologetically.

"That's okay," Leona replied. "I'm not really in the mood for coffee anyway, and I surely don't need anything to help me stay awake."

"Tell me about your son," the chaplain replied.

"I suppose I sound angry," Leona replied, "but I don't have much patience tonight, and I'm too upset to talk much."

"I don't blame you. I'd be upset as well."

"Mickey was like most kids—they all want to have friends and be the hotshot and all. Well, Mickey thought the way to do this was to have a motorcycle. He bought it with his own money. Believe me, that's all he had. But the friends you attract with a motorcycle aren't the type I wanted Mickey to hang around with. You know—bar hoppers and loose women. Now this happens!"

Leona looked carefully at the chaplain and decided he had no idea what she was talking about. She didn't want to create the impression that her son was out of control, even though he was at times. So she changed the subject.

"You said you wanted to pray with me. Well, if you still want to do that, go right ahead."

The bewildered chaplain fumbled around starting a prayer, and Leona realized he was inept at this situation. She remembered carrying a prayer in her purse that a friend had given her and pulled it out.

"I've got one that I say with the visiting committee at church," Leona offered. "It's pretty good."

Relieved, the chaplain nodded that Leona should go ahead and read the prayer.

Leona quietly prayed that God would help her Mickey but at the same time acknowledged that everything was in His hands. She said she would accept His will, whatever that might be for Mickey. She recognized that God did not always do what she wished but rather would do what was best. She had full confidence that God would look after Mickey, and her as well, one way or another.

At the end of the prayer, Leona could see that the chaplain was surprised. *I guess he didn't expect that an old woman would know how to pray—or for that matter trust God!*

Two hours later, the doors to the operating suites finally opened, and two doctors in green scrubs approached Leona. Somber and weary from the prolonged surgery, they looked up at her.

"Mrs. Ward, I'm Dr. Floyd, and this is Dr. Brennan. We've just finished surgery on your son, but he's still being worked on by Dr. Simpson, a neurosurgeon, and Dr. Campbell, an orthopedist."

"How's Mickey? Did he make it through everything okay?"

"Mrs. Ward, your son lost a lot of blood, partly due to a ruptured spleen. He has swelling of the brain from the head injury, and Dr. Simpson is draining blood to reduce the pressure. The orthopedist is still waiting to set his broken leg and fractured pelvis. He has not regained consciousness since the accident, so we can't yet determine his brain function. Although his heart is beating fine and he's being ventilated properly on a respirator, we are most concerned about possible irreversible brain damage. Only time will tell."

Leona's face turned downward as she heard the news. A million questions raced through her mind, not knowing what to ask next. A sense of doom and helplessness overcame her as she drifted from the conversation. "He wasn't awake when he arrived at the hospital?"

"No, he was unconscious, and we won't know for several days whether or not he'll recover. He'll likely be in the operating room for another hour and then will be moved to the surgical intensive care unit. You should be able to see him then. I'll be checking on him frequently and will update you on his progress as we find out more."

She had more questions but the words stuck in her throat,

and Leona found herself alone in the OR waiting room. Even the chaplain had managed to disappear, but Leona didn't mind being alone. Instead, she pulled a small Bible from her purse and paged to Psalm 23. The words were too small to read, but she had this psalm memorized, so it didn't really matter. Softly she said to herself, "The Lord is my Shepherd. I shall not want." She continued reading the passage and praying that Mickey would be okay.

A nurse tapped her shoulder. "Mrs. Ward, your son has arrived in room ten. You can follow me, and I'll take you to him."

The hospital lights had been dimmed for the night, and the halls seemed exceptionally quiet and bare. The dark, somber walk down the hall contributed to the gloom that Leona felt.

Leona followed the nurse, passing the nurses' station where staff were busily charting vital signs, observing cardiac monitors from a central location, and finishing preparing medications for their individual patients. She passed rooms where patients lay covered with bandages on their heads, abdomens, or chests. Many were connected to respirators, heart monitors, IV tubes, and other devices that Leona had only seen in television soap operas.

When she finally arrived at Mickey's room, she didn't recognize her son. His long blond hair had been shaved except for a small portion on the right side. A strange tube protruded from the top of his head and was connected to a monitor that measured intracerebral pressure. Bandages crossed his abdomen, and his leg was suspended in the air, lying on sheepskin and traction devices. About the only skin that Leona recognized was around his biceps, displaying a black barbed wire tattoo. Leona took note of the endotracheal tube coming out his nose, which connected Mickey to the ventilator and provided the rhythmic breathing movement on which he now relied.

"Mickey," she called gently. "It's your mom."

Mickey neither blinked nor flinched, so Leona slowly stroked his warm body.

"Mickey, you're a good boy. I'm here to care for you. You're going to pull through this. I know you will. The nurses and doctors are going to take good care of you, but I'll be here too. I know you want to sleep, but I love you, and Jesus loves you too."

Again, Mickey made no response, and tears welled in Leona's eyes. The nurse put her arm around Leona and said, "Mrs. Ward, Mickey is sleeping now, and sleep looks like something you could use."

"My son is fighting for his life—how could I possibly sleep?" Leona responded.

"Well, I'm not sure you can, but I can bring you a blanket and you can rest in the waiting room. I'll let you know if anything changes, but Mickey's stable right now."

Leona turned and buried her face in her hands and sobbed. "I can't believe it! He just has to pull through this!"

The nurse copied Leona's home phone number and got a brief history of Mickey's allergies and past illnesses. She obtained appropriate consent forms from Leona and then led her back to the waiting room and returned Mickey's meager belongings to her: a set of motorcycle keys, a Timex watch, a black plastic comb, and a well-worn black wallet with faded pictures of Mickey's old girlfriend.

Leona's life was about to change.

CHAPTER 4

Music blared in Nick Seratino's ears as he read the sports page. Even above the music he heard, "Nick, Nick! You've got an important letter." Pulling out the ear buds, he yelled to his sister Teresa, "Okay, I'm coming."

Slipping on his tennis shoes and bounding downstairs to the kitchen, he found on the large central island a large stack of mail including bills, advertisements, and junk mail, but separated from the pile was an official-looking letter addressed to Nickolas Seratino. He recognized the gold embossing as the letterhead of Providence University. He had, after all, received a rejection letter from them only two weeks ago, so he was curious what this could be now.

He read:

Dear Mr. Seratino:

In our previous correspondence to you, your admission to our university had been denied. However, you were placed on the alternate admission list. We are now pleased to inform you that you have been promoted to acceptance into the university for the fall semester. If you plan to attend our school, please complete the enclosed enrollment forms and return them to us at once so we can arrange housing and class schedules.

Congratulations on your admission, and we hope to see you in two weeks.

Sincerely,
Robert Tannenbauer
Director of Admissions

Tossing the letter nonchalantly into the stack of other mail, he surmised that he would eventually get accepted into Providence, the school of his father's choice. Things always seemed to go his father's way, and this acceptance was no exception.

"Nick, what was that letter?" Teresa asked as she came into the kitchen. "Did you win the lottery?"

"Don't I wish! No, actually, it's an acceptance letter from Providence. I guess they finally saw the light and are letting me in."

"Nick, that's great! Isn't that where you wanted to go?"

"It's where Dad wants me to be, but it'll be okay—I hear they have fantastic parties."

"You'll get to see Selena every day. Hey, where are you going? Aren't you going to stay and tell Mom and Dad?"

"Look, you tell them for me, okay? I promised John I'd meet him over at Heroes in a few minutes, and I'm late. Thanks, Teresa."

The black Cherokee roared out of the driveway, and the whole neighborhood could hear the cranked-up Rockford

Fosgate amplifier, blaring rap music through his MB Quart speakers.

Just as his music faded out of range, Emilio and Rosa Seratino entered the kitchen, and Teresa eagerly told them the news. "Mama, Nick got into Providence after all! He just got a letter today."

Rosa responded, "Really? That's great! Where's the letter? And where's Nick? Was that Nick's doing, or yours, Emilio? I hadn't heard you mention anything about Providence."

"Are you questioning my son's ability?" Emilio replied smugly.

"Don't play games with me. This is just too much of a coincidence to have happened out of the blue."

Emilio indifferently shrugged.

৫৩

"John, how are the Bulls doing?" Nick yelled as he strolled into Heroes Bar.

"Pretty good considering Jordan's not with them anymore. So what's up?"

"Just got a letter saying I got admitted to Providence University," Nick responded nonchalantly."

"Really? Hey, that's incredible. How did you manage that one?"

"It just pisses me off—not that I don't want to go there, but I'm guessing my dad got me in—my sister's there and all. She'll probably be more upset than I am. I mean, she got there due to her brains, and here I am—I'm probably there because of my daddy. Makes me feel real good, not earning my own way," Nick scoffed.

"I have to admit, Providence isn't quite your style. But hey, how could your dad manage something like that?"

"He's got friends. He won't talk about it much, and I've learned to not ask. Hey, did Joel come through with my new older and wiser driver's license version? I can't wait to be 'twenty-one.'"

"You got it, buddy. Bit of trouble getting it to look authentic, but it looks pretty good now. Take a look." John pulled the card from his back pocket and handed it to Nick.

"Wow, it looks great. Thanks! This little card will be just my ticket for partying at Providence. How about we break it in, to celebrate my getting in, say tonight at nine?"

"You're on!"

CHAPTER 5

Leona Ward had spent the week following Mickey's accident at his bedside and in the waiting room, reading her Bible and greeting her children, who had stopped in to visit their brother. Leona's faith had seen her through rough times in the past, and she routinely turned to the Lord for help on a daily basis. She prayed quietly to herself in the ICU waiting room, a drab and sterile setting feeling very much like what she would have expected the operating room to have felt like to Mickey. Coffee was available, but the chairs were stiff and upright. In one corner slept a family member waiting to hear news on his loved one. One window allowed sunlight to pierce the room, giving some warmth to an otherwise cold environment.

"Dear Lord, if it is Your will, please restore my Mickey to health." She trusted the Lord and knew He would provide her the strength and comfort to face whatever lay ahead. With an alcoholic husband who left her and two sons who were drug addicts, Leona was acquainted with struggles on a daily basis.

Dr. Floyd had visited her several times during the week,

but despite the fact that Mickey's vital signs were stable, Mickey appeared to be lifeless on the respirator. He remained comatose, and his only movement was a periodic flinch of his extremities. The nurses tried to present the overall situation as optimistically as they could, but Leona knew things were grim. By the end of the week, Leona had begun to recognize the hopelessness of Mickey's condition, so when Dr. Floyd called her at home and asked to meet with her on Friday, Leona prepared herself for the worst.

When she arrived at the consultation, Drs. Floyd and Brennan approached her with somber looks. Their faces told her what to expect. As they spoke, Leona's mind wandered. She heard them speaking, but it was as though this was a bad dream.

"Mickey survived his accident, but unfortunately, he'll never wake from his coma. His EEG continues to be abnormal. In short, Mickey has had serious brain damage, and we don't expect he will ever regain consciousness. It is our recommendation that you consider allowing us to turn off the respirator and withdraw all life support. He is in a vegetative state and will never be normal. He is, essentially, dead. Brain dead."

"But, doctor, wouldn't that be like killing Mickey? How do I just stop everything? What do I do now? I was afraid you would tell me it was hopeless. How long do you think he can keep this up?" Leona asked.

Leona heard what was said, but it was the last thing she wanted to hear. She had prayed so hard and had hoped that God would heal Mickey.

"We can breathe for him and keep his heart beating, but complications will ultimately set in, and Mickey's heart will stop. If there was any hope of recovery, we'd love to tell you so, but there is really no hope here. We do think there is some good that could come out of all this. With your consent, we could take Mickey's kidneys, heart, and liver and donate them to someone else. Right now, these organs are still working properly."

"What do you mean, someone else?"

"There are many people waiting to receive a donated kidney, heart, or liver because they have organ failure. There are many people dependent on dialysis. We could transplant Mickey's kidneys, and two people with kidney failure could live a more normal life by giving one kidney to each person."

"A kidney transplant? Gee, I don't know. I've just never thought of such a thing. Can't anyone do anything for Mickey? Dear God, I know my son's a good kid, just give him one more chance! Mickey was never sick. Never went to the doctor, but he never had any money or insurance. " Leona sobbed as she buried her head in her hands.

Did God fail me? she thought. *I know He's always with me, and I did pray that I would put everything in His hands. I just didn't want this to be the outcome. What do I do, God? I need your guidance. Send me some sign about what to do?*

After the doctors left, Leona pulled Mickey's wallet out of her purse. Through tear-filled eyes she found his driver's license ... and there it was, the sign she was looking for. Once she saw the signature to allow organ donation, she knew the answer she would give the doctors. Her often-irresponsible son had done at least one responsible thing. He had signed his driver's license for organ donation.

CHAPTER 6

The Delta Xi frat party at Providence University was slated to start at ten p.m., but as usual, that was when the first students began arriving.

In the few weeks Nick Seratino had been on the campus, he felt pretty good. He was aware that all the girls were noticing his wavy black hair and good looks. Every coed seemed to flirt with him, and his ego was soaring, so tonight Nick wore his designer Italian clothes because he wanted to set himself apart from the usual college dress of sweatshirts and jeans. His new BMW that his father had bought him was quite a contrast to the older Fords and Chevys in the parking lot of the fraternity house.

Nick made it to the party about 10:30 and noticed right away a good-looking blonde in one corner of the room. When her eyes met his, he gave her a wink, and he saw her blush. Trying to fill his beer glass from the keg while looking at her, he spilled beer foam and beer on his Cole Haan shoes, and she laughed when she saw what had happened.

"Hey, is that any way to treat a poor guy who's new on campus?" Nick asked in a relaxed tone. "You could have offered me some help."

"Well, do you need some help now?" the blonde responded with a demure smile.

"No, I'm fine, but maybe I could help you. Would you like a cold beer?" the experienced womanizer asked. "My name's Nick Seratino, in case you're interested."

"Sandy. Sandy Miller."

Soon the two were dancing to the beat of the live band that had been hired for the evening. The beer and liquor flowed freely at the fraternity house, even though this was clearly against university policy. Nick retreated to his special stash and brought vodka and water for them to drink. And as the alcohol began to take effect, they both felt giddy.

"So what year in school are you, and what's your major?" Nick asked.

"I'm a junior with a double major in English and chemistry," Sandy responded.

Naïve, Nick thought. *Just the type I was hoping to find tonight.* "Great! Then you can write a novel about the periodic table!"

Nick and Sandy danced throughout the evening, and when the party ended, each had downed about four beers plus the vodka. They danced closer as the night went on, and Nick periodically gave her a kiss on her neck. His hands drifted up her back and slid across her chest when she turned. He knew she liked this attention because she never objected to anything he did, but he could tell she was getting tired.

"Well, if you're going to be 'out on the floor,' I'd prefer it's be in my room rather than this crowded place," Nick teased. "By the way, I'd like to show you my room. It's right upstairs, and maybe we could unwind a bit in private."

His plush room was a contrast to the usual frat house accommodations. Surround-sound stereo. Flat-screen TV.

Soft loveseat. New oak desk. Mini fridge. Queen-sized bed with designer bedding.

"I know what you're thinking. Well, you have to know the right people," Nick said with a grin.

"And tell me, who are the right people?" Sandy asked.

"I can tell you who the right person is right now," Nick whispered as he pulled Sandy into his arms. He deftly clicked the remote, and Frank Sinatra's voice began to sing "The Way You Look Tonight." Nick gently fondled Sandy's erect nipples and skillfully unhooked her lace bra. Time passed quickly, and they drifted off to sleep.

Nick woke up feeling her naked body next to his.

"Hey, it's time for you to go home now," Nick muttered sleepily. "Sorry, Cindy" (or was it Sandy?). "The frat rules say no girls overnight," Nick said as he rolled over to fall back asleep.

She angrily jumped out of bed, grabbed her clothes, and stomped out of the room.

After she left, Nick staggered out of bed toward the bathroom. He had a splitting headache from all the beer, and his bladder felt like it would burst. He relieved himself, and as he flushed the toilet, he noticed blood in the stool. *Great,* he thought. *She didn't tell me she had her period.*

CHAPTER 7

As Nick walked into his home for Christmas vacation, he smelled the spaghetti sauce simmering on the stove.

"Wow, this smells great," he called out before grabbing a bite of an apple left on the counter. Before he was able to greet his mom, he felt suddenly nauseated and ran to the bathroom and promptly vomited.

"Nick, what's wrong?" Rosa asked.

"Aw, nothing. Probably partied too much," Nick responded.

"I'm going to have Dr. Rossini see you while you're home on break. You look lousy."

"Mom, don't worry. I'm fine. Look, I've made it through my first semester, and now that I'm home, I don't want to waste my time seeing some doctor. I want to celebrate making it through the first semester! I passed most of my classes, but Providence is really tough, you know."

"You mean there are classes in doubt? Did you get a tutor?"

"Look, Mom, you know as well as I do that getting into

Providence probably was Dad's doing. It doesn't really matter what kind of grades I get. I'll probably end up working for Dad, and he couldn't care less about my GPA."

"Nickolas, you need to do your best. Don't get an attitude of mediocrity. Look at your sister."

"Which one? Selena? Don't compare me to her. I'd die living like her. I could never stare all day at the books like she does, so don't expect that to ever happen."

"We all have our talents, and I know you can you do well in school."

"Dad never even finished high school, so why are you bugging me about grades in college?"

"Because you're capable of doing well and shouldn't throw away these opportunities. Besides, you can't fool your mother. I think we need to have Dr. Rossini take a look at you. I'm going to call and make an appointment, just to make sure."

"No, Mom, I'm fine. Let me rest for a few days, and I'll be all right." Nick knew that regardless of what he said, his mother would call the doctor anyway.

"Where is everyone else?" he inquired.

"Lorena and Tim will come over on Christmas Eve. Tim is having problems at the grocery store with the meat cutters. I guess they're threatening to go on strike. Horrible timing right at the holidays."

"And where are my sisters?"

"Teresa, Olivia, and Catherine should be home from their dance lessons any minute. They can't wait to see you."

"I'm at least a role model to someone. Actually, I've missed them too, but don't tell them. I don't want them to get a big head. How about Selena?"

"I thought you would know. You do go to the same university, don't you?" Rosa asked sarcastically.

"You know I'm not like Selena—I don't go near the chemistry lab. My only chemistry is the one of beer and women, and I'm not doing that great in that category right now, either."

"Nickolas, shame on you. Don't talk like that. You need to focus on school. Your father is so proud that you're at Providence."

Just as Nick began to respond, Teresa ran into the kitchen. "Nick, great to have you home! Can you give me a ride to the movies? I'm meeting my friends there at eight, and Mom and Dad are babysitting Lorena's children, Antonio and Maria."

"I thought you were happy to see *me*. What's this about heading off right away to some movie?" Nick asked.

"No, Nick. It's great to see you. But I do have someone I'm meeting at the movies," she whispered into his ear.

Rosa left to take Nick's laundry to the utility room.

"Do Mom and Dad know about this? You're only thirteen if I remember correctly."

"You won't tell them, will you, Nick? Please!"

"You owe me one for this, understand? Okay, I'll take you. I can drop you off on my way to John's house. I'll be ready to go in about an hour, okay?"

Nick stopped the BMW, his new ride that his father gave him for getting into Providence, at the front door, and Teresa hopped in. They sped off down Poplar Street, and Teresa began applying makeup. It was going to be hard to get Teresa to the movie on time, so Nick was trying to hurry.

God, I'm sleepy, Nick thought as he rounded the curve.

Teresa's screams woke him as she jerked the steering wheel clockwise to avoid hitting the oncoming car. The BMW swerved to the right, and the right front fender struck a parked car. The deployed airbags stung their faces, and Nick felt sharp pain in his nose. They heard the screeching of bending metal as the front end of the car crumpled and smoky air filled the car.

"Nick, what's wrong with you? You nearly got us killed!" Teresa cried.

Nick, trembling and perspiring, asked how Teresa was doing and then gingerly touched his swollen nose. "I can't believe it. I must have dozed off. Mom and Dad aren't going to be happy about this one. My nose is killing me. I wonder if I broke it. Find the cell phone and call the police while I check with the other car and see how they're doing."

The police arrived, and they did a breath analysis on Nick and then sent him to Deaconess Medical Center in an ambulance with Teresa accompanying him.

Nick was examined in the ER, and the nurses contacted Dr. Tony Rossini, the Seratino family physician. Facial X-rays, a urinalysis, and a CBC and chemistry profile were ordered.

When Dr. Rossini arrived at the emergency room, Emilio and Rosa Seratino were just coming in the door.

"Tony!" Rosa called out when she saw Dr. Rossini. "We're so glad you're here."

"Rosa, I'm so sorry to hear about Nick. They haven't given me any report. Let me check on him, and I'll be right back."

Dr. John Beamer, the ER physician on duty, told Tony that the facial X-rays looked fine and that the nose swelling would probably go away in a day or two. It was doubtful that the nose had been fractured. Instead, John was concerned about the hemoglobin of 8.2 mg% and the blood and protein in Nick's urine. He ordered a sonogram of Nick's kidneys.

"That is unusual, John. He's really anemic, with a hemoglobin of only 8.2gm%. You know that a normal hemoglobin is 12–14gm%. What do you think is causing his anemia? There isn't a splenic injury? Does he have a kidney contusion?" Tony asked.

"The sonogram should tell us that, but it looks more like a chronic disease to me."

"His mother wanted me to see him in the office next week, so maybe he hadn't been feeling well."

"Hold on, Tony, look at this chemistry profile." He handed the lab report over. "This kid's got full-blown kidney failure. Maybe that's why he fell asleep at the wheel. We have to admit him."

Tony Rossini walked grimly into the ER waiting room and addressed Emilio and Rosa. "Nick is a sick young man. He doesn't have a broken nose, but it looks like he has kidney failure. I'm contacting Dr. Adam Foster, a nephrologist, to see him."

"A nephrologist?" Emilio asked.

"A kidney specialist. He's the best in this field."

"How could a car accident make his kidneys fail?" Emilio asked.

"It didn't," Tony responded. "This has been going on for a while it seems."

CHAPTER 8

Slightly overweight senior transplant surgeon, Dr. Howard Potwin, strolled into the conference and addressed the attendees. "Ladies and gentlemen, our preeminent transplant program at Deaconess Medical Center has been one that others have tried to emulate. In the past, our community has worked with our hospital leaders and backed our efforts financially, and thus, we have been able to establish the outstanding transplant center that we have today.

"There are three distinct areas I plan to discuss tonight: kidney retrieval, use of living donors for transplantation, and cadaveric transplantation. As you know, several young patients on dialysis are awaiting a transplant. I believe the number is more than one hundred at present. The kidneys often come from patients who are declared brain dead, and our trauma service promotes donations after discussing it with the injured patient's family. In the past year, we have retrieved kidneys from thirty patients, with each patient providing two kidneys apiece for a total of sixty kidneys.

"Not all these kidneys can be used locally. In some cases,

no appropriate match can be found. In other situations, the federal law, which established UNOS, the United Network for Organ Sharing, requires us to send kidneys to other locations where there is greater need. As a result, of the sixty kidneys we retrieved, only twenty-three were transplanted into local recipients.

"Because of the length of waiting time for a cadaveric kidney, most institutions are beginning to focus closely on a living, related-donor program. In the living-related transplantation scenario, a kidney is removed from a healthy relative donor and is transplanted into a recipient, usually a close family member.

"I recommend that we begin promoting more living-related transplants and that a fund be established to hire transplant coordinators to oversee this program. We also need to assure that the recipient of a transplanted kidney takes the appropriate medication to avoid rejection of his new kidney. Therefore, the fund could help purchase antirejection drugs for the indigent. Since the mortality rate of dialysis patients is nearly ten to fourteen percent yearly, we could greatly improve survival by increasing the number of transplants performed.

"Establishment of the Deaconess Transplant Fund will enable us to get local as well as national recognition for our excellent program. This fund could be financed by corporate as well as private donations and would benefit those patients as well as the hospital. If you have questions, I would be happy to visit with you further about this after the end of tonight's meeting." Potwin smiled broadly and reveled in the loud applause following his speech.

The group enthusiastically decided that it would be important to promote the fund and donor consent on driver's licenses. Within the week, he had heard that the news media was pushing the fund and that the donations had started pouring in. It was just the edge they needed to stay on top.

CHAPTER 9

Dr. Eric Strong heard his cell phone chirp that he had a message. Long gone were the pagers and now cell phones were the method to connect with other doctors and patients. Strong was a tall, handsome transplant surgeon and Potwin's partner. He was still single but was dating a smart graduate chemistry student. *Hmm,* he thought. *I normally don't get calls from Tony Rossini.*

Strong dialed the number, "Hey, Tony, what can I help you with?"

"Eric, I have a problem patient, a nineteen-year-old male who is also a family friend that I admitted last night. He came in after a car accident. We didn't find any serious injuries from the accident as far as we can tell. Instead it looks like he has kidney failure, probably chronic. He's anemic. Hasn't been feeling well for a while. I called you because I know this family will be pushing immediately for transplantation. Can you see him this morning? His father can be difficult, but Nick's a good kid. Being nineteen, he's scared to death and hasn't been telling his family how ill he's felt."

"Sure, Tony. No problem, but we need to get Adam Foster

involved too. He is going to need a nephrologist. You know I can't just pull a kidney off the shelf."

"Tell that to his father. He always gets his way, if you know what I mean. Let me know what you think after you meet him."

∞

Eric hung up and entered the dialysis unit to check on one of his favorite patients waiting for a transplant. As usual, the room had a constant hum from the thirty-two machines running continuously. An elderly patient in the first recliner was lying back with his feet pointed upward in shoes that should have been replaced ten years ago. He had an odor from rarely showering, but this was partially offset by an acidic odor that was present from the chemicals used to clean the machines.

Sitting next to him was a middle-aged woman struggling to knit, restricted by the needles in her arm for dialysis. In the third chair was the district attorney whose briefcase was partially opened and papers scattered over his lap so he could review his recent court case.

The lights were turned up bright so the nurses could keep a close eye on everyone. Four rows of patients sat in recliners, some sleeping, some reading, and others watching television.

"Well, Derrick, how did you do this weekend? We're still looking for the right kidney for you. Santa hasn't shown up yet with the package, but I know he will."

"I felt better, Doc. I didn't drink as much and was able to work two shifts down at Barney's, but I had to drop out of school this semester. I couldn't keep up with school, work, and dialysis. I really hate it. You know I have to go to school if I hope to be a doc like you."

Eric furrowed his brow because he liked Derrick and

had wanted this young, attractive African American male to succeed. Derrick came from a single-parent family and had avoided the drug and delinquency problems that had plagued his brothers. His grades were above average in high school, and he had received a scholarship for college, but it came at a time when he first noticed symptoms of kidney failure. His blood pressure was a problem in addition to his nephritis, and the start of dialysis was another setback toward his goal of wanting to be a physician. He had hoped to go to medical school, but now with kidney failure, he felt his future was doomed.

"I'm sorry about that, Derrick. I can contact the school for you and assure them that your health wouldn't prevent you from returning next semester. You know it would be a shame if medicine was denied a great brain like yours. Listen, when you get that transplant, you'll be good as new. Don't give up hope. Let me know if I can help you in any way."

Moving to the nurses' station, Eric stopped to see the nurse manager. "Any other patients I should visit while I'm here, Nancy? I wanted to check on Derrick. He's lucky if he knows where his family members are, let alone talk to them about kidney donation. I don't think any of them would qualify anyway—they're into the drug scene pretty badly. His grandma's about the only one he even talks about. Yeah, I think all of us would like to tell God a few things about who should and shouldn't get sick. But I'm optimistic about getting him a transplant. I hope one turns up soon for him. Any other patients I should talk with now?"

"No, you're good for now, but I hear we may have another young patient here."

"It looks like it. I'm going to see him now."

Making his way back to the hospital, Eric went to the seventh floor to see Nick. He stopped at the computer to look over his records and noticed that Adam had already seen him, concluding that his renal failure was likely a form of glomerulonephritis. Since he had small kidneys, he didn't think it would be helpful to do a biopsy.

"What can you tell me about this kid?" Eric asked the nurse.

"I think you need to know more about the parents. That father can be a pain in the butt. Look, I'm sure he means well, but he's difficult. You'd think we had no other patients in this hospital.

So Tony was right. This family is going to be difficult. Wait a minute. Seratino. I'm dating Selena Seratino. Surely they can't be related. She's avoided having me meet her parents.

Luckily, Emilio had left Nick's room to get lunch so that Eric could examine his new patient without a barrage of complaints from the father.

Staring at Nick's face, he said, "That's quite a nose you've got there. I'm Dr. Eric Strong. Dr. Rossini asked that I come by to see you regarding your kidney problem. Do you have sister named Selena? We've been dating for a while."

"So you're the Casanova she's talked about. Yeah, she's the brainy one in our family. We don't see each other much on campus because she's always studying. I spend more time in the frat house. I heard the doctors think I have a kidney problem, but I have no idea what they're talking about."

"Well, your lab reports indicate your kidneys aren't working, so we need to check it out. Have you noticed anything wrong with your urine? Like has it been brownish in color, cloudy, or bloody at all lately?"

"Well, it might have been bloody one time, but I don't make it a habit of looking much at my pee."

"Any pain when you urinate?"

"Nope, doesn't hurt."

"And has the urine been brown or foamy?"

"Like I said, I don't look much, but it has seemed a little brown. And about the foam—I figured foam in, foam out! Isn't that what happens when you drink beer?"

"Not really. In fact, foam is a sign of protein in the urine. So have you felt bad?"

"I've been a little tired lately, but I've probably been hitting the parties a bit too much."

"Have you been sick to your stomach?"

"Doesn't this happen to every college age kid? You drink too much and then you're sick the next morning. Sure, I've thrown up a few times."

"Has it happened even when you don't drink?"

"I guess I have puked a lot in the mornings, but after that, I feel okay."

"The sonogram you had this morning shows your kidneys are small, and your blood tests show they aren't removing all the waste products and toxins from your system. That's probably why you've been so tired and nauseated. This, combined with your history of possible blood or protein in your urine, leads me to think you have Bright's disease, also called glomerulonephritis."

"Globular nephritis?"

"Glo-mer-u-lo-nephritis. It's a disease that can silently destroy the working tissue of your kidneys and gradually, over time, you lose all kidney function. In most cases, patients don't have any symptoms until their kidneys have failed."

"But wait a minute, I still pee."

"Sure ... sure you do, but the quality of urine that you make isn't very good. That's why the kidney poison level, the creatinine, and BUN are now high, and that's why you feel bad."

"Great! Now I'm being graded on the quality of urine I produce, and I'm not getting an A in this subject either, right? Okay, so what do you suggest?"

"Nick, I'm being serious here, your lab results show that you need to start dialysis."

"Dialysis. Isn't that where they hook you up to a machine?"

"Well, there are two types of dialysis, but basically yes, it's a way of filtering and cleansing your blood—and the type of dialysis I'm recommending we start is hemodialysis, so you would be hooked up to a machine."

"That's something for old people—I'm young! I don't want to be on dialysis."

"I don't blame you, Nick. But we really don't have a lot of choices here. The toxin levels are so high in your body that they are making you sick. I don't mean to scare you, but your kidneys have failed, and that's a serious problem. Dialysis seems to be the only option right now."

"Both kidneys have failed?"

"Yes, both."

"Wouldn't I stop making urine? I can't believe this. Look at me. I don't look sick, do I? How long would I have to be on this dialysis?"

"Each dialysis treatment is adjusted to fit each individual patient, but the average time is around three to four hours three times a week. Dialysis is basically your artificial kidney for the rest of your life."

"For the rest of my life? No way. This has got to be a joke—I can't be on dialysis all my life. You've got to be kidding."

"I wish I were, Nick, but I'm not. There are other people on dialysis who are your age. It's not limited to those older."

"Yeah, I can imagine—they're probably all scrunched up and all—not like me. I'm healthy. Can't you see!"

"I'm not here to argue. We need to get your toxin levels down or you'll not be able to return home at all and could die. Let's see ... I have here that you are about nineteen. That means you can consent for the procedure, but I want your parents to be aware of the problem before we get started. I think you'll feel a lot better once you're on dialysis."

"I'm going to talk with my dad and Dr. Rossini about this."

"Absolutely, I want to talk with them too. Your parents need to fully understand the treatment we're prescribing. But we need to start dialysis soon—like this afternoon."

"You know I still pee; this doesn't make sense. I mean, here I am, I had a car accident, hurt my nose, and you say I have to go on dialysis, even though I still pee. I admit I haven't felt all that great lately, but isn't this a bit drastic? And if I try dialysis once, does that mean I have to keep it up? You're the doc here, but man! I'm not ready to hear something like this!"

Nick paused, and tears filled his eyes. "I mean, I've got to think about it a bit. I might try it once and see how it works. But just once, you understand."

"We'll try it once, and then discuss the future. But I'm sure you'll feel better."

"Does it hurt bad, Doc? I'm sort of scared, and I don't want anyone around to see me like this."

"No. It's not much different from how you'd feel giving blood. I'll stop in and check on you while you're on the machine. You'll do fine, I'm sure."

Emilio and Rosa walked into the room. Rosa greeted Nick with a big hug, carefully avoiding his swollen nose.

"Mom, Dad, this is Dr. Strong—he's a kidney doc that Dr. Rossini called in."

"I'm Eric Strong, a transplant surgeon. I've wanted to

meet you, actually. I've been dating your daughter Selena, but she hasn't introduced us."

"She did mention you," Rosa responded. "And she has talked so positively about you. I had hoped to get to meet you also."

"I've gone over the details of next steps with Nick, but let me tell you as well. He needs an access for dialysis, and we'll start the treatments this afternoon."

"No other alternative?" Emilio asked.

"Nick is a good candidate for a kidney transplant, but we have to take things one step at a time."

"Would that mean no dialysis?" Emilio eagerly responded. "If we can avoid dialysis, that's what we'll take."

"Like I said, we've got to take things one step at a time. Yes, a transplant would eliminate the need for dialysis, but that option is in the future. Right now we've got to get Nick's electrolytes and toxins back to a safe range, and dialyzing him is the only way we can do this."

"Well, do what you must. I guess Nick can sign his own permission forms, but he's a special kid, and we only want the best for him," Emilio said. "We've got to get him back in top shape—don't we, Nick?"

Nick didn't answer but instead slipped out of bed and raced to the toilet to vomit.

Eric happened to have a lighter schedule that day so he was able to work Nick into the operating room schedule with ease. Eric met Nick in the preop area.

"In order to perform dialysis, we need to be able to access your bloodstream, so we need to insert a catheter here in the neck area as a temporary connection. Then we can filter and clean your blood with the dialysis machine. Later we may need to place a permanent access in your forearm that will be ready to use within a few weeks. This will give us time until we can get you a kidney, which hopefully will be soon."

"Where did you say you were going to put that tube for dialysis?" Nick asked. "I can't have hoses hanging out of me."

"It's not quite that big a tube," Eric said, smiling. "Actually, the catheter is placed here, right below the collarbone. It's temporary, and it will lie flat under a shirt. Later we will insert a permanent access here, in the left forearm if you're right handed."

"Why don't you put in the permanent access right away? I want to get this show on the road."

"We plan to insert it within a few days, but we can't start using it for about three months anyway. It takes that long for the vein to enlarge so we can easily insert needles," Strong responded.

If Nick hadn't been fully nauseated before the discussion, he certainly was so now. "Needles? Oh hell, do what you have to do," he replied weakly.

Emilio called Dr. Rossini from Nick's room.

"Hey, who is this Dr. Strong? Did you call him in on this case? He's in there seeing my son now."

Dr. Rossini recognized Emilio's panicked voice. "Calm down, Emilio. Dr. Strong is an excellent doctor. He's not the oldest doctor in that surgical group, but I think he's a talented young doctor."

"Well, who is the oldest doctor in the group? Did you know Strong is dating my daughter?" "Really? Strong is a great physician, but Dr. Potwin started the group. He's our age, but Strong is doing most of the cases now."

"I want to talk to Potwin, then. I don't trust having some

new smart aleck taking care of my son, even if my daughter likes him."

"Dr. Potwin will say the same thing as Dr. Strong, I'm sure."

"Maybe so, but I should get to hear from the top dog."

"Are you saying you want Dr. Strong off the case?"

"No. Hell, I don't know what's best, but maybe an older doctor would be more experienced. Strong's putting in some tube now, and I don't want to delay something Nick needs. I want to be sure that we're certain that this is the best way to go."

"Why don't we leave things as they are, but you can call Dr. Potwin for reassurance tomorrow. Would that be okay?"

"You bet I'll call him. He needs to know that we expect more than just run-of-the-mill care. We're the Seratinos, you know."

CHAPTER 10

Eric got the panicked call from Selena. "My brother is really sick, isn't he? I feel terrible. I've been ticked at him all year because I thought that he should never have gotten into Providence and my father pulled some strings so he could attend. He doesn't study and parties all the time. It made me mad that Dad always favors him, and now I have this guilt trip since he's so sick and I wasn't paying attention to him."

"Look, Selena, you wouldn't have been able to tell. Kidney failure is a subtle problem that can sneak up on the person. He was gradually worsening and didn't know it."

"But I should have known," Selena said. "I've been around him, and you'd think I could see he wasn't the same."

"Sometimes it's easier to notice these changes when you're not close to the person. Look, we'll take good care of him. I'm going to make every effort to find him a kidney soon."

Eric realized the Seratinos were having trouble adjusting to the fact that their son had kidney failure. He hated seeing anyone dependent on dialysis, but finding the problem this late left no other options.

He entered the well-prepared operating room to insert the dialysis access catheter and observed that everything he needed was already in place. Nick was on the procedure table with sterile drapes covering his chest and head. The catheter, gauze, and anesthetic were accessible on the surgical stand near the operating site.

"Nick, this is Dr. Strong. I know you can't see me with that drape over your head, but I'll explain each step to you so there will be no surprises. You'll first feel a small pinprick and a bee sting sensation from the local anesthetic. Then I'm going to tip your head down to insert the catheter."

ᘒᘓ

Nick was still groggy from the premedication he had received and flinched very little from the local anesthetic. In a matter of twenty minutes the catheter had been inserted, the position confirmed with fluoroscopy, and Dr. Strong was suturing the catheter in place to secure it from moving or slipping out. The drapes over his upper chest were removed, and Nick was wheeled back to his room. The sedative he was given was still in effect, and Nick felt dizzy as he studied the ceiling of the hospital corridor during the ride back to the room.

Within an hour of the catheter insertion, Nick was wheeled to the dialysis unit on the sixth floor of Deaconess Medical Center. Nick gingerly slid into the bed beside the dialysis machine at one of the eight stations in the acute dialysis unit. The room itself was not large, and four other patients were currently being dialyzed at other stations.

Through blurry eyes Nick saw a sterile room with other beds placed next to machines that had pumps turning. Other patients lay in beds beside him, but they appeared alert.

Shaking from the chilly operating room, he turned to see an attractive nurse standing beside him.

"Nick, I'm Amy, and I'm here to do your dialysis treatment."

Nick shrugged with a half-hearted smile.

She weighed Nick and took his blood pressure and vital signs. She placed a mask across her face, applied gloves to both hands, and then removed the caps from the dialysis catheter. Tubes were then matched from the dialysis machine with the red-capped end attached to the red end of the new catheter and the blue-capped end attached to the blue end of the catheter. The blood pump was turned on, and blood began flowing through the tubing and gradually through the dialysis filter attached to the machine.

Nick listened as Amy explained that the dialyzer had hundreds of tiny tubes that the blood flowed through but that the blood stayed inside the tubules and was returned to the body. She told him the waste products would leave his blood and diffuse into the dialysate solution in much the same way tea flows into a glass of water yet the leaves stay in the tea bag.

Nick tolerated the dialysis very well. Three and a half hours later, Amy disconnected the tubing from his access, and Nick was returned to his room.

Thank God that's over. I guess it wasn't as bad as I expected. With the drugs I had, I don't remember much of it. I wonder what has become of my car? Am I going to fail in my classes next semester if I can't get to all the lectures? Can I get my dad to help again? I really don't want him to manipulate things for me.

"Nick, how'd it go?" Emilio asked, entering Nick's room.

"It wasn't as bad as I thought it was going to be dad. In fact, I'm a little hungry, and I haven't felt that way in a long time."

"That's great! I'll have Mom bring you something to eat ... a little home cooking after a long day."

"Are you okay? I've been worried sick about you," Selena asked as she entered the room.

"Well, look who's here," Emilio responded. "The surgeon's girlfriend."

"Look, Dad, Eric is a great guy, and I'm sorry you had to meet him like this. He's going to do all he can to help Nick."

Dr. Foster entered the room. "Your first treatment went pretty well. Your electrolytes and blood pressure are falling into normal range. How are you feeling?"

"Fine, as far as I can tell. I actually feel better now than I did earlier today."

"We'll need to dialyze you again tomorrow. Do you have any objections or questions about that?"

"It's not what I want, but another treatment won't be so bad, I suppose."

"Good, we'll see you tomorrow. I need to tell you that you'll be on a few diet restrictions while on dialysis, and you'll be limited to about a quart of fluid each day."

"Diet restrictions? Hell no! I'm not going to change what I eat or drink. I'm facing enough right now."

Foster said, "There's a lot of things happening to you all at the same time, but yes, there are diet changes you'll need to make. For example, you'll have to give up pizza and bananas for a while. You see, with the kidneys not working, you'll have to curtail some of the foods that could give you problems. I'll have a dietitian talk to you and your mom."

Emilio added, "They can talk all they want, but I'm telling you that Nick is going to eat for a change. I found out that he's been throwing up for days, and now you say he's got to be on a special diet?"

"Treating your son is a cooperative effort," Adam said.

"If he drinks excessively, he's going to pay for it the next day. We try to allow some foods he likes, but they're going to have to be taken in moderation. What more can I say? I'm having a dietitian come talk to you." And with that, Dr. Foster left.

Poor dietitian, Adam thought. *If Emilio's in the room, she'll feel like a fish that's been released in a piranha tank.*

Once Nick was released to the general floor, the hospital halls were flooded with his friends, each professing that they were his dearest friends who would never let him down. John came with a pepperoni pizza from Sal's Spot, and Jeremy brought in a liter of Coke. Nick enjoyed the attention and actually ate more than he had in weeks. Maybe this dialysis thing wasn't going to be so bad after all.

CHAPTER 11

*T*oo *many things to think about. Too many things to do.* With bags under his eyes from a poor night's sleep, Emilio grabbed some coffee. *I need caffeine to think straight.*

"Rosa, I'm calling a different doctor to see Nick," Emilio announced.

"What for?" Rosa asked with concern.

"I called some of my friends, and they told me there's a guy named Potwin who's been there longer and is more our age. You know, more experienced."

"Emilio, we haven't given Foster and Strong a chance."

"It's just that they're so young. Not enough years under their belts. We didn't pick these doctors, Tony did. Tony didn't even know Nick was getting sick until he showed up at the hospital. You should have seen Nick last night. Eating your food and loving it. Rosa, he looks back to normal."

"I'm glad he liked the food."

"Sure did. Now it's time to get a second opinion."

"Where did you get Dr. Potwin's name? What does he have to do with Nick's case?"

"He's the head of the surgical department that handles that kidney transplant thing and access insertion and stuff," replied Emilio. "And we want to talk to the head guy,"

"But I thought we had Dr. Strong doing that. Do we want two doctors working on the same thing?"

"We'll have ten doctors working on Nick if it helps, Rosa. Yeah, Dr. Strong is working on it, but I thought the oldest and most experienced doctor in the group should have a look at Nick too. Don't you agree?"

"In most cases I do, but we haven't even seen what Strong can do, and he seems like such a nice man. I trust him."

"We haven't switched doctors yet, but I decided we should hear from the top dog!"

"Imagine how that will make Dr. Strong feel," Rosa retorted.

"Now's not the time to worry about a doctor's feelings, Rosa! I've already got it all set up." *She's not going to change my mind. I know what's best for Nick, and I'm the only one around here who gets things done. She should be glad that Nick liked her food. After all—her place is in the kitchen.*

GᘒᕲD

Emilio paged Dr. Potwin and had the amazing luck of having him answer the phone directly.

"Dr. Potwin, my name is Emilio Seratino, and my son started on dialysis yesterday with your partner, Dr. Eric Strong. I wanted to talk with you about my son's condition."

"Dr. Strong doesn't prescribe dialysis, he's a surgeon. If you have a son who's a patient of Dr. Strong's, why not talk to him?" Potwin answered matter-of-factly.

Controlling his temper, he dismissed the cold response. "My son, Nick Seratino, has developed kidney failure, and the doctors don't give us much hope other than saying he'll be on dialysis the rest of his life unless he gets a kidney. Now, we know you're one of the head doctors at Deaconess, and we wanted to make sure Nick was getting the best treatment."

"You said his name was Nick Seratino?" Potwin asked, suddenly taking more interest.

"Yes, my son is Nicholas. The doctors say he's got Bright's disease and will have to be on dialysis all his life."

"He's about twenty?"

"Nineteen to be exact."

"He started dialysis recently?"

"Just yesterday, and he's still at Deaconess. Would you look at him and tell us what you think? My wife, Rosa, and I would really like to hear from an experienced doctor."

"I normally don't get involved with other doctors' patients, Mr. Seratino, but I'll check in on him at your request. Were you having a problem with Dr. Strong?"

"Not really, it's just that my wife and I are not too experienced in the medical field, and we want the best treatment possible for our son. We thought you were more experienced, that's all."

Emilio hung up feeling slightly more relieved. *Doesn't hurt to kick a little butt,* he thought. Hell, to him anything he could do to help Nick was worth the time, and Rosa's reluctance wasn't going to stand in the way. Emilio knew how to accomplish things, and he intended to get what he wanted.

CHAPTER 12

The Seratinos drove to the Medical Plaza Office Building next door to Deaconess Hospital in their black Mercedes. The plaza building had gleaming terrazzo floors and quiet, wood-paneled elevators that were appointed with lovely landscape paintings. Emilio located the directory and discovered that Drs. Strong and Potwin's offices were both on the third floor.

After exiting the elevator, Emilio turned to Rosa. "Let me take care of this. I think I can get these doctors in gear so Nick can get this transplant."

"Don't worry, I don't plan on saying a thing," Rosa responded sarcastically.

Rosa had worn her fur-collared black cashmere wool coat but removed it in the waiting room, revealing a tailored cobalt-blue suit. She was an attractive lady with deep reddish brown hair and gorgeous blue eyes, the same colors that her son, Nick, had the good fortune of inheriting. She had not gained the weight so typical of many women in their fifties and had maintained an attractive figure.

The nurse led Emilio and Rosa into the meeting room and

seated them at the end of a long oak conference table. Eric Strong entered shortly after and asked how Emilio felt Nick's first dialysis had gone.

"Fine," Emilio responded, "as far as dialysis treatments go. We don't want this long term, however."

"Neither do we," Eric responded. "No one wants dialysis, but it will allow Nick to resume many of his normal activities. In Nick's case, we think the best long-term solution would be a transplant, and that's what we should talk about today.

"There are two basic types of kidney transplantation," Eric began. "In one type, the kidney comes from a person who is brain dead—that is, he has no brain function left, but the heart is still beating and other organs are still functioning. The numbers of kidneys we receive from these donors don't match the number of patients needing a kidney transplant, so these patients have to wait until kidneys become available. Then once a kidney is available, the kidneys have to be matched to the recipient. In the meantime, the recipient is kept alive and well on dialysis. The amount of time the recipient has to wait averages about one to two years, but of course sometimes people are lucky and get a transplant sooner. Others haven't been as fortunate and have had to wait longer."

"We would want one right away, Dr. Strong," Emilio interjected, who actually thought this was the end of the conversation. "We can afford to make sure Nick gets one this week, if you know what I mean."

Eric understood what Emilio was trying to say but thought it better to ignore the comment and continue on. "Not every type of blood donated matches every person needing blood. Similarly, not all donated kidneys match the recipient."

"Sure, Doc, I get it. We don't want a run-of-the-mill kidney. Not just a kidney from anyone off the street. We want a perfect match from a stud for Nick, don't we? Italian would be the best," Emilio added.

"A perfect match would be ideal, but it is often quite rare," Eric explained. "But there is a way to improve your chances of getting a better match."

"Like stacking the deck, so to speak?" Emilio asked. *Now he's starting to talk my language. Maybe this guy's better than I initially thought.*

"I hadn't really thought of it in that way," Eric mused, "but it is sort of like stacking the deck. I'm talking about someone in your family donating a kidney to Nick. The chances of a closer match are higher if the kidney comes from a blood relative. And you only need one functioning kidney to survive. Moreover, matching doesn't apply to skin color or gender. It could be a perfect match from an African American, a female, or any nationality."

"Great! So you're saying his sisters could be a donor. I know that any one of our family members would be happy to give Nick a kidney, wouldn't they, Rosa?"

Rosa hesitated for the slightest of seconds, at which Emilio said with exasperation, "Of course they would! They've got a spare! Isn't that what you said, Dr. Strong? They keep one and they donate one."

"How old are your daughters? We often don't accept kidneys from children."

"Well, three of our daughters are still in school, but Rosa or I would give one. So would Lorena or Selena. They're Nick's older sisters, and they would be happy to give their brother a kidney."

"This is a conversation that needs to take place with them directly. They may worry that they might someday need a kidney for one of their children."

"Okay, so Lorena may have more children, and who

knows, maybe she's pregnant again, but there's Selena. She just wants to be a researcher. She probably won't have children. Oh, wait a minute, that's right—you're her boyfriend. Hey, maybe she'll do something right and have children."

Eric rolled his eyes. "Mr. Seratino, you can't decide for your whole family, anyway. We have to get their consent. Plus, they have to agree to be tested."

"Oh. Of course! But I can assure you that we'll all be willing to donate. How do we get this done?"

"We will contact the family members and have them come in for blood work to check for cross-matching."

"Fine. We can get you the girls' phone numbers so you call them today. Right, Rosa? Oh wait, let me guess—you don't have any of their numbers with you. You see, my wife can be very disorganized."

"Look, I don't take the information anyway, Mr. Seratino. That's arranged through the organ bank, and they certainly won't get around to it any sooner than this afternoon."

Rosa was embarrassed and angry that Emilio had talked this way in front of Dr. Strong. She and Emilio left the conference room, and Rosa pulled a hanky from her purse. As they walked down the hall, they passed an older doctor who looked at them in a perplexed manner. Rosa nearly covered her face with the hanky as he passed.

"Rosa! Don't make a fool of yourself crying!" Emilio chided as Rosa dabbed away the tears.

CHAPTER 13

The hospital and the surgical ICUs had become very familiar territories to Leona Ward. Visiting hours had just been announced, and Leona walked slowly and deliberately toward the electric doors into the ICU. Leona was accompanied by her oldest daughter but asked her to wait in the hall. Leona wanted her last conversation with Mickey to be in private. She was relieved at her decision but still could not tolerate the thought of saying her final goodbye.

"Mickey, they say you can't hear me, but just in case you can, I'm telling you that I love you. I've decided to donate your kidneys because I saw that's what you wanted done. Mickey, I wish to God it were me lying there, not you. You had so much life left to live. But at least you're not in pain. It's me who has the pain, Mickey. I'm in pain because I don't want to let you go. If you do anything, anything, then pray 'Jesus.' There's power in His name. I've prayed for you many times a day since your accident. I've done all I can and so have your doctors. I'll be okay, so don't worry about me. I'm proud I'm your mom. I always have been. I love you, but I have to let you go. God, I wish this weren't happening. Mickey, I decided I'd donate your kidneys—and your corneas, for that matter. I mean, you won't need them anymore, and maybe someone else could use them. When you see Jesus, it won't be with earthly eyes anyway. I wish I could go with you. What better place could there be?"

And with that, a tearful but resolved Leona Ward kissed him tenderly on the cheek and left the room.

Eric Strong was in Max Strickland's room when he received the page from Dr. Floyd. He was explaining the procedure for declotting the access to an irritated Max, and the page seemed like one more unwanted distraction.

"This is Dr. Strong," he said into the cell phone as he stepped aside. "Oh hi, Mike. What's up? ... Yes, I'm free this afternoon after I finish this declotting case. So tell me about this kidney donor. ... Oh man, that's tragic! Those motorcycle accidents are awful! So how long has he been like this? ... Yeah, and you said his mom has given consent, right? It sounds like he'll be a good donor for us. Thanks, Mike. I should be by to see him within an hour. ... Okay, and I'll call you when I'm finished."

Turning back to Max, he said, "Sorry about that disruption. So you think you understand the procedure?"

"Sure I understand. I've only been through this five times before! Why doesn't this damn access stay open? Did you put it in right?"

"Listen, we hate to have it clot off, too. I don't know why you're having so much trouble with it clotting. We have you on an anticoagulant. Maybe your blood pressure is getting too low. I'll talk to Dr. Foster about that. You know, I really do understand it's the pits having to be declotted so frequently."

"So it sounds like there's going to be a kidney available for someone. Why not cancel this declot thing and give me a kidney transplant instead?"

"I don't make those decisions. You know it's determined by a waiting list and by cross-matching and all. You're a lawyer, and I know you know the legal aspects of this."

"So who's up for the next one? Is it Mildred?"

"I wouldn't know. It'll be the one that matches the best."

"The law always has a loophole, doesn't it? Hey, look, let's just drop this conversation and get on with the declot. I'm tired of this whole thing and have a lot of stuff to do this afternoon. I need to get out of here."

Nick Seratino was incredulous at the logic of the hospital nurses. He had been shaving in the tiny compartment that was the patient bathroom and had walked the halls of the hospital wing all morning, yet when he was to dialyze early this afternoon, he had to wait for an orderly to wheel him to the acute unit. He wasn't nearly as frightened about the dialysis treatment this time and was perfectly calm when he arrived at Station Two.

"So, Mr. Seratino, let's just have you step on the scale and see how much you weigh," his nurse instructed him.

"Fine," Nick replied as he wrapped the hospital gown around him tightly to cover his bare essentials and stepped onto the scale. He was secretly glad that the unit seemed to be so hidden from other areas of the hospital. He couldn't imagine having any of his friends seeing him like this.

The nurse recorded the weight and checked on the

previous day's post-dialysis weight. "My word, Nick. You've gained eleven pounds! How did you manage that?"

"You're acting as though eleven pounds is a lot of weight. How would I know how I gained it? I didn't pee much last night. The machine's supposed to take care of that for me, isn't it? It's probably this towel."

"Well, yes, but this is a higher than expected amount of weight for you to gain. How much water did you drink?"

"Who counts? I didn't throw up last night. That probably explains the weight gain. First night in a long time that hasn't happened."

"I'm happy about that too, but you have to limit yourself as to how much fluid and salt you take in. The dietitian has talked to you, right? And you're on a renal diet, aren't you? Let me just check the chart here."

The nurse quickly flipped through the small chart and smiled as she located the signed orders. "Says here renal diet, all right. That's strange."

Nick felt uncomfortable about the nurse's obvious suspicions and said, "Look, I eat, and you take care of the rest, and we'll get along fine here."

"I'm going to have the dietitian visit with you again. The rules and guidelines are for you, not us. You'll feel better, and your dialysis runs will go smoother if you stick to the rules. Are you sure you didn't drink more than four glasses of water since yesterday?"

"I told you, I didn't count! This whole dialysis thing sucks!"

The nurse ignored the last comment and proceeded to take Nick's blood pressure. She wasn't surprised that it was 150/110 mm Hg. "Your fluid problem is reflected in your blood pressure too. Too high a blood pressure is hard on your heart."

Nick felt he had heard enough lecturing for the day and said with exasperation, "Yada, yada, yada. Just put me on the machine, would you?"

（）

Selena hurried back to her dorm after just completing her analytical chemistry final. Most grad students lived off campus, but she found being the resident assistant on the floor gave her close proximity to her classes plus the seclusion of her own room to study.

"Selena, there's an urgent message from your Eric," the receptionist said as she passed the front desk of her dorm.

Oh my God. Nick is worse. I'll never be able to forgive myself. Dumping her notebook on the unmade bed, she quickly called Eric's cell. After three rings, he answered.

"Eric, what's going on? Is Nick all right? How did the dialysis go?"

"Nick was doing better after his first treatment, but I'm not sure about today. Adam watches that. I wanted to talk with you about the meeting I had with your parents. You dad is really something, isn't he? He's going to hit you up about being a kidney donor. Actually, for that matter, he's going to hit everyone up about being a donor. He seems to think you're a good candidate because you're a career woman, but he threw me a bone today now that I'm in the picture because he believes you might have children. Up until now he thought you would be an old maid."

"My gosh. So he thinks we're engaged? Now you understand why I was reluctant to have you meet him. I'm not surprised that we all have to be at his bidding for the favorite child. He stops at nothing to get what he wants, and right now, that something is a kidney for Nick."

"Selena, you didn't tell me Nick was feeling bad last semester!"

"I didn't realize he was sick. Actually, I told you I should have checked on him. Quite frankly, I was irritated that Nick had been admitted to Providence in the first place. But I can't change that now, and I'm sorry. I feel guilty about not checking on him. Now I suppose I'll feel guilty if I don't give up one of my kidneys."

"Whoa, I didn't know you would be so upset about this meeting. Let's just take it one step at a time. There are going to be many options for Nick, and we're just getting started. I know what I'm doing here, and I can guide you through this. Your dad only thinks he's in control. Much of this is beyond anyone's control."

"That's what worries me."

"Ahhhh!" Nick screamed, piercing the silence of the typically quiet dialysis unit. "My leg. It's killing me!" he yelled as he grabbed his calf.

"Nick, I told you there'd be consequences to your high fluid gain," the nurse chided.

"You mean cramps like this occur on dialysis? Damn this hurts! Do something to fix it now!" Nick cried out.

He could almost feel the pain melt away after the nurse gave him calcium. Looking around the room, he noticed another patient stare back at him as though nothing unusual had happened.

Hell, hasn't he ever had a cramp? That smile looks more like a smirk—the smirk of someone who gets his kicks out of watching someone else suffer, Nick thought. Nick feigned a grin and glanced at his watch. He realized he had two more hours to go.

You schmuck, he thought as he stared the other patient down.

Nick arrived back to his room, where his mother was waiting. "I'm fine. I'm just fine."

"You don't lie very well. Now what happened?" Rosa asked.

"All the medical people talk the same! Hell, I drank too much! And it was water at that. But I got it straight now, okay? The dietician is going to talk to you. I guess she needs to let you know that I can't have all that salt. That's what they tell me."

Nick knew he hadn't eaten the prescribed diet but hated to go through another lecture, so he hesitated for just a second.

His hesitation was Rosa's chance to speak up. "She's talked to me, and I know now. Low salt, and less foods that have potassium, like tomatoes. Less fluid. I've got it."

So much for a normal life. Blah, blah, blah. Don't eat this. Don't eat that.

"Nick, I didn't know I was doing anything wrong, but we need to make these changes."

"All right, I get it too. I'll try to stick to this, but it isn't going to be easy. I wonder how much potassium is in a beer."

CHAPTER 14

Leona Ward watched a pair of somber orderlies roll Mickey Ward's body, the ventilator still attached, out of the ICU and toward the surgical suites. When she saw the ventilator tube her heart stuttered, because she knew what was about to happen.

She sat in one corner of the waiting room with her head bowed and prayed quietly. She knew this was the last day Mickey would be with her on earth.

Mickey was taken to surgical suite number one, and Dr. Strong was busy scrubbing for the upcoming operation. A surgical resident was going to assist, and the transplant team was waiting with the incubator to accept the kidneys.

Mickey's body was carefully lifted onto the table, the ventilator still breathing for him. His abdomen was prepped with Betadine, and a sterile drape was spread over the surgical site. The anesthesiologist managed the ventilator and monitored Mickey's vital signs to ensure that the kidneys would continue to receive blood and remain healthy.

Eric was handed the scalpel. He made a midline incision to reach the kidneys. He dissected down to the kidneys until the renal artery and vein were identified. The kidneys were both a healthy pink, and Mickey was making a large amount of urine because the anesthesiologist had given him a large bolus of normal saline solution. Within forty-five minutes both kidneys and his liver were removed. The incision was closed, and the ventilator was discontinued.

Eric watched Mickey's heart rate begin to slow, eventually changing from a normal rhythm to a sine wave that slowed, flattening to a straight line. No heart sounds could be heard, and Mickey expressed only two agonal breaths as his life left him and his color transformed to the ashen pale white of death.

Mickey Ward had officially died.

Although Nick felt that yesterday's treatment was an experience from hell, he noticed that he felt better today. His appetite was definitely improved, and even the bland hospital breakfast tasted great. Emilio and Rosa had arrived early with Selena, and Nick noticed how truly beautiful his sister had become. Nick was happy to see her, and it occurred to him that none of his college buddies had made any effort to stop by. Nick's daydreaming was interrupted when the six-foot frame of Dr. Eric Strong appeared in the doorway.

"I heard from the nurses you were singing in dialysis yesterday—or maybe I should say screaming. Look, you're not the first person to learn about dietary restrictions the hard way, but it's a lesson you rarely forget in the future. Your treatment today will go better."

"Today. What do you mean today? I just had a treatment yesterday."

"When you first start dialysis, particularly in the hospital, we dialyze you daily until we get to a steady state."

"Oh, great, just what I wanted to hear."

"I've gone over the transplant options with your family, and I know Adam has reviewed dialysis with you. I think he mentioned home therapies, but with school going on right now and our intent to try to find you a kidney, I think your decision about in-center dialysis is a good one. Your sister and I will make sure we get your dialysis treatments scheduled around your current classes. Right, Selena?"

"Yes we will, and I'll be a better big sister. I'm not letting you out of my sight."

"That's not exactly what I wanted to hear. After all, Nick's an adult and will learn to take care of himself. But maybe for now, both of us won't let you out of our sight."

Selena blushed for a moment but smiled, saying to Eric, "I'll give you plenty of attention. Jealous of my kid brother, huh?"

Nick interrupted. "Look, I'll take all the attention you two want to give me. Just give me a break from Dad. Oh, and by the way, you notice that I don't see any of my college friends here."

"That's true. None have shown up, but that's not surprising. College guys can't deal with situations like this. Nick, we need to go over the fistula, so let me explain. It will be a minor operation where we connect an artery in your arm to a vein in your arm. Over time, the vein will get larger, and this can eventually be used for the connection to dialysis. Two needles will be inserted into this vein,"

"Wait a minute. Every time I dialyze I have to have two needles in me? I'll look like a druggie. It's bad enough to have this hose sticking out of my chest. Needles hurt!"

"Well, the tube in the chest will be taken out once

you start using the access in your arm, but I'm sure Dr. Foster mentioned there is another option for you, which is peritoneal dialysis. I would place a tube in the abdominal cavity. Fluid is instilled through this tube and remains in the abdomen for a few hours and then is drained off. While the fluid sits in the abdomen, it removes the toxins that have accumulated because your kidneys are not working. We would teach you how to perform peritoneal dialysis at home."

"Not exactly my idea of a great menu here," Nick commented, relieving some of the tension the whole family was feeling. "This surely will be better. It doesn't take needles, does it?"

"There are no needle sticks into the skin in this one. However, it is rather time-consuming."

"Like how time-consuming? Is it four hours three times a week like hemodialysis?"

"Peritoneal dialysis is done daily, not just three times a week. There are four exchanges each day, and each treatment takes about forty minutes to complete or it can be done overnight with a machine that cyclers the fluids in and out."

"Let's see. There's four exchanges times forty minutes for a total of 160 minutes, or over two hours just doing the exchanges. That's not so great. And could people see this catheter tube? And where would I go while I was doing this procedure?"

"Listen, Nick, our ultimate goal here is a transplant, but until we get to that point, we need to get you feeling better through dialysis. The hemodialysis is usually done in a center, although it can be done at home as well."

"I can't imagine running this whole process at home. I think sticking to the center dialysis is the best answer for me," Nick responded. "The nurse does the treatment for you and you go home. Perfect. I don't have to mess with anything myself."

"You don't have to do the procedure yourself, but it does require that you restrict the fluid, salt, and potassium in your diet like we talked about, or you'll have the problems like you had yesterday. The peritoneal dialysis has the advantage that it can be done at home, or in your case, at school. It's very gentle, and it preserves your own kidney function for a longer period, though it also carries a risk of peritonitis."

"Peritonitis! What in the world is that?"

"It's an infection in the abdomen that occurs if you're not careful handling the catheter and fluid. You see, the bacteria love this warm, sugary fluid and can grow rapidly in the dialysate. It requires meticulous care to keep things from getting contaminated and infected."

"Which type of dialysis would be best considering we hope to get Nick a transplant soon?" an astute Selena asked.

"Either type would be satisfactory, but hemodialysis would be slightly less time consuming, considering it would be performed only every other day. Both types of dialysis have their pros and cons."

"You said, 'preserve kidney function.' I thought you had said his kidneys had failed. What do you mean by preserve function?" asked Selena.

"Nick has a tiny bit of kidney function left. That's why he was still urinating before the accident, but the kidneys were not filtering out the electrolytes adequately. In initial peritoneal dialysis, the patient may still urinate some."

Emilio interjected. "Does all this stuff really matter anyway? Look, our whole family has agreed to be tested for donation. Surely you'll have a match from a couple of us, and in a few weeks, your life can get back on track."

"That's probably right, Dad. Besides, I don't think I want

to do that home business. I have too many things to take care of, and I don't want to be bogged down with messing with a treatment every day. I just can't think of poking myself with needles—someone else can do that, but I can't."

Nick realized a tear was streaming down his cheek, and Rosa discreetly handed him a tissue.

Eric said, "I think that would be a good decision for you, Nick. Our chronic dialysis unit is right across the street, and you're welcome to visit it anytime. There's a patient your age there named Derrick Jones, and I think you two might get along great. I'll arrange to have an access put in soon if you're sure that hemodialysis is the type of treatment you'd like."

"Okay, but I need to talk to you alone. Is that okay?"

"Sure. They can step out so we can talk."

"I need to be here. Say anything you want in front of me, Nick. You're my boy."

"Listen, Dad, I need to have this conversation alone."

"Oh all right, go ahead. But you don't have to any secrets from me."

After they left, Nick timidly began to talk. "Doc, what about sex? You know I'm young, and I can't give up everything."

"You could have problems with erections, but we'll see. If you do, I can help you with that."

"Can I ever have children?"

"Certainly, if you get a transplant, and even possibly on dialysis. But you're a long way from wanting that, I presume."

"Sure, but you know, these things just keep coming to me."

"I understand. Let's just take one thing at a time."

ೞ

Dr. Strong was able to arrange the fistula insertion that afternoon, and Nick was soon back in his room awaiting discharge from the hospital. He was glad the surgical site was covered for the time being. He couldn't tolerate seeing what an access would look like, and he figured he would have plenty of chances to look at it later.

Emilio and Rosa had gone home, and he was alone for a while when he got a visitor from the dialysis unit. Derrick Jones had come to see him at Eric's request, and Nick was surprised that he was black and moreover that a dialysis patient would look so healthy.

Derrick was relaxed and able to put him at ease in no time. He told Nick about various people in the unit and agreed to introduce him around when he comes to dialysis on Monday. Although Nick probably wouldn't have picked Derrick as a friend prior to his illness, Nick was happy to have at least one person his age going through a similar experience that he could talk to. And here was, a total stranger, taking time to visit. It was something none of his college buddies had bothered to do. He was learning quickly who his true friends really were.

Selena gave Nick the ride home after he was dismissed. Emilio and Rosa had a little homecoming party planned for Nick, and Rosa had tried cooking the meal meticulously following all the dietary restrictions. Lorena and Tim brought over the items from the grocery store, and the family all cheered as Nick walked into the house.

Nick had to admit it was great having such a supportive family, and he especially hugged Teresa, who had sense enough to grab the wheel and avoid a head-on collision just a week ago. He was amazed that Lorena had consented to be tested for kidney donation as well. After all, he knew this sister was a busy mother yet was willing to give part of herself to give an often-ungrateful brother another chance at a normal life. Tonight he wouldn't complain once; he was just happy to be home.

CHAPTER 15

E ric was in the doctors' lounge having a cup of coffee before doing a procedure. The lounge was the perfect place for the doctors to vent all their complaints about the hospital, the nurses, reimbursement from insurance, or the lousy food they had gotten in the hospital cafeteria. There was a soft couch, a few recliners, and bland decorations but a tray of pastries to have with the coffee.

His phone rang. "Dan, what is it? You don't normally call me directly. Oh, I see. These are instructions from higher up. Let me guess, Tuttle called you. Potwin too? As in my *partner*, Potwin? Okay what is it? Tissue typing is back already? You're kidding. Huh. You were told this had to be stat? I get it. So what're the results?" There was a longer pause. "What? Only the mother matches? That doesn't make sense. What about the father?" Another pause. "The father doesn't match. A total mismatch! Hang on, let me write this down."

Eric grabbed a pen and his notepad. "Yes, I'm ready. The father is A2 A24 B15, 45 C6, C7 DB4,13 DR3, DR1,DQ2,3. Son: A23, 26, B49, 58 C4 C5 DR12, 15 DR2 DR4 DQ1, 6. Are you sure this is right? There are no matching antigens.

Total mismatch, like you said. The son should have some of the genes from his father but there aren't any. Oh wow. So Emilio isn't the father?"

Do I tell him—or for that matter, how do I deal with my girlfriend, his sister? I wonder if she knows. I doubt it. Hmm. I wonder if the mother knows. You would think she might suspect that her husband isn't the father, but she probably doesn't know for sure.

Eric shook his head, listening to Dan further explain. "Tuttle wants me to get back with him? This should be a shocker. Why should we treat this person any differently than anyone else? The national media already thinks the wealthy fare better than the average Joe, and I've prided myself in acting fairly to everyone. Sorry, Dan. I'm a bit cynical, but this family is driving us all crazy. My job is to see that the hospital would deal equitably with everyone. I'll call Tuttle in a moment. I'm not mentioning this paternity business. We have enough problems already with this family. Thanks for the call."

Eric thought about Tuttle. He'd been reasonable to work with in the past, but money talks. Image and financial outcomes were the CEO's main focus now. Playing by the rules seems to be second place. *No reason to delay the call,* Strong thought.

The secretary answered the phone after only two rings. "Administration."

"Angie, this is Dr. Eric Strong. Could I talk with Mr. Tuttle?"

"Sure, Dr. Strong. His next meeting isn't for another fifteen minutes so you've caught him at a good time. Just one moment."

"Dr. Strong, it's good to hear from you," Tuttle began.

"I understand you want an update on the Seratino cross matching," Eric responded dryly.

"Yes, yes. Emilio Seratino has been very influential in our community, and I've heard that he chose Deaconess for his son's care. We surely want to see that his family is not disappointed, so I took the liberty of calling in extra help to speed up the cross matching process. The results should be in by now, or at least that's what they've told me."

"Mr. Tuttle, isn't it unusual to focus on just one of Deaconess's patients? Nick Seratino actually is doing well, but it looks like he'll be a chronic dialysis patient until we're able to get him a transplant. Unfortunately, I just heard that none of his family members either match or qualify to be a kidney donor except for his mom, and she's probably diabetic, so that rules her out as well. Mr. Seratino will have to recruit more relatives for testing."

"Oh—that's not good news. But of course, at Deaconess we'll be able to get him a transplant fairly soon, I'm sure. Dr. Potwin just gave a great talk about our transplant program the other night, and now we have a high-profile person to be a recipient. This is just great! I can see the headline: Deaconess Medical Center gets kidney transplant for local executive's son."

"The Seratinos aren't exactly celebrities, Mr. Tuttle, but did you hear me say that none of the closest family members match or can donate? That means the son gets put on the cadaveric transplant list just like the rest of our patients awaiting a transplant."

"Is the family aware that they don't match?"

"No, I was told that you wanted to be called first. So here's the call. I plan to arrange for them to come to our office."

"And what do you think the time frame will be for him getting a cadaveric transplant?"

"Once he goes on the list, we're looking at one to two years. It could take even longer."

"Why? Deaconess is supposed to be one of the leaders in transplants, and you'd think they could get this kid one sooner—that would be a real feather in our cap, you know?"

"Looking good isn't necessarily following set protocol, Mr. Tuttle. I mean, sure, we hope Nick's match occurs sooner, but we can't skew the rules for one person just because he's from a wealthy family."

"It's going to be hell for us once Emilio finds out there's no match."

"But we can't withhold this news from him, either. We'll have to put up with whatever he throws our way."

⚭

Tuttle had never considered that Nick couldn't get a transplant right away. *I'll be damned if I'm going to let this promotional opportunity for Deaconess pass me by*, he thought as he dialed Howard Potwin.

"Howard, this is John Tuttle. I've just spoken with Strong about the tissue-typing results on the Seratino boy. He tells me only the mother matches the boy, and she can't be a donor because she may be diabetic. I'm concerned that the father will go berserk when he finds out his son could have a long wait on a cadaver list. What can we do?"

"That's horrid news as far as I'm concerned, but has everyone been tested fully?"

"I think so. I guess I didn't ask that. But I was sure hoping that we could get this kid some help right away. Times are tough in so many hospitals, and this transplant program seemed to be one thing that was going right. I was counting on it giving us some needed publicity, at least."

"Plus this is a young man we're talking about here. It'd be hell to be nineteen and on dialysis. Look, John, the transplant list isn't public record by any means. Maybe I can move him up a bit myself. No one would ever have to know but us."

"Eric Strong would probably figure it out, wouldn't he? And he's the most likely one to object. He's so into ethics and all."

"Look, Eric's my employee, not my partner. I can take care of him. Just trust me a bit here. I agree with you; we can't just sit tight on this one. Getting the Seratino boy a quick transplant could make or break our program."

ᏻᎧ

Nick Seratino entered the outpatient dialysis unit and wiped the cold sweat off his forehead. *Thank God, there's Derrick,* he thought as he slipped off his leather jacket in the waiting room lobby. "Hey, Derrick. What's up, buddy?"

"Not much, dude. After all, we're in the dialysis unit, man. Not exactly the hot spot of Chicago."

"You're not kidding. With all these needles into veins around here, I'd have thought we were in drug city. Seriously though, how's it goin'?"

"Good, man. Basically boring. It just takes some adjustment, but the people here are pretty nice. It's the time commitment that gets you. Three days a week in this place gets old really fast. Come on in and I'll introduce you to a few of my friends here."

Derrick took Nick from station to station. He met Max Strickland, who grumbled a few words under his breath, muttering something to the effect of "another prisoner."

"Derrick, how old is that guy? He's so wrinkled and grumpy. Does he ever smile? His baggy clothes seem much too big for him, and he's just what I expected to find in this place."

"They're not all like Max. He always seems to have a

chip on his shoulder. I guess he was quite the lawyer in his day. Loved going after people for whatever he could get from them, but his crotchetiness didn't help with relationships. He's been divorced three times."

Nick met Evelyn Jones next, a sweet sixty-five-year-old housewife who seemed to be the mother figure for everyone younger than her. Jess Thompson, an overweight diabetic who was arguing with the nurse about his recorded weight gain sat next to her, and Tina Parker on the end was a forty-two-year-old waitress who had been on dialysis five years because of recurrent kidney infections. Several other patients were already connected to the machine, and more were waiting to begin.

"Is this a dialysis unit or a dinosaur's unit?" Nick kidded when he glanced across the bay of patients.

"Hey, don't judge the book by its cover. Things could be worse. Without dialysis, these people would be dead, including me, so watch what you're saying," Derrick responded.

Nick pulled out an iPod and put in his ear buds so he could listen to music while he waited to start on the machine. He looked over at Derrick, who had picked up a magazine and was casually looking at the pictures. It occurred to Nick that Derrick had no such source of music.

"Want to listen to my iPod?" Nick asked.

"Thanks, but I'm fine. I like to snooze during the treatments anyway. Helps the time pass."

"Yeah, I suppose it gets old quickly being here," Nick responded.

"Not as bad as you might think. I sorta like talking to all the patients. You can learn a lot from many of them. Everybody has a story to tell, if you just take the time to listen."

Nick resurveyed the diverse group. "Adds new meaning to motley crew, if you ask me," he replied. "Gawd, I hope this doesn't take long. I don't think I'll last long here."

"The name of the game is *transplant*. That's our ticket out of this joint. And everyone is clamoring to get one. See Evelyn over there? She's been waiting about two years now. No kidney in sight."

Nick changed the subject. "So what do you do when you're not here dialyzing?"

"Oh, I work at Barney's. You wouldn't know the place. It's just a tiny drugstore, and I work there about four days a week, probably more now that I had to quit school."

"Why'd ya quit school?"

"I couldn't balance work, school, and dialysis all at the same time. Plus, my family's a mess. Lordy, you wouldn't believe all the stuff they do. I actually enjoy working so I can establish my own life, if you call this living."

"Hey, I'll have you up to my frat house sometime. The guys have been giving me a bit of the cold shoulder there, but we can hang out. I think I've got more in common with you than I have with some of them."

"Which frat house? You know I'm not exactly going to fit in with the high-class crowd."

"You fit in with me, and both of us don't exactly fit the mold of these patients either," Nick replied. "We'll see what I can work out."

"Or you could help me tomorrow at Barney's," Derrick replied. "Expose the elite kid to the real part of town."

"Sure thing, Derrick."

৩১

The Seratinos arrived at Eric Strong's office, and the secretary escorted them to a conference room where she offered them coffee or sodas.

Soon Dr. Strong entered the room and could sense the

tension among the Seratinos. He took a position at the head of the table.

"Okay, Strong, what did the tests show? Which one of us has the matching kidney?"

"Mr. Seratino, I'm afraid I have some bad news. It appears that only your wife would be an adequate match for your son, but she does, in fact, have high blood sugar, and we need to have her see Dr. Rossini as soon as possible. We test for diabetes in individuals who are being evaluated as kidney donors because we know diabetes can cause kidney failure in some people, and we don't want to jeopardize the donor's health. Her kidney function is normal now, but she'll need all her kidney function in the future. We feel she should not be a donor."

"So Rosa is diabetic? Hell, what more bad news can you tell us?"

"Please, Doctor," Rosa interjected. "I'm not concerned. I would gladly donate a kidney anyway."

"Mrs. Seratino, I'm afraid with your medical problems, it would be too risky."

"Do you mean my diabetes makes it risky for me or for Nick? I'd do anything for my boy. If my kidneys are working okay, I'd be willing to do with just one, or would he become diabetic too?"

"Your kidneys are working okay for now, but diabetes can slowly damage them, so you're going to need both kidneys yourself. Dr. Rossini will be notified about your diabetes, and you'll have to follow up with him."

"Great job, Rosa. Just when you could have helped your son, you have to show up with diabetes! You sure I don't match? I'm healthy as a horse!" an exasperated Emilio Seratino yelled.

"It was a bit of a surprise that no one matched Nick in your family, Mr. Seratino, but sometimes that's the case," Eric said with caution. "It looks like we'll have no other alternative than to get your son on the cadaver transplant list, but we could consider a donor who is not related. In the meantime, we'll complete the transplant workup and place him on the cadaver transplant list, so as soon as a kidney becomes available, we can give him a transplant."

"And hope the right person dies? That's just great! What time frame are we looking at? One to two months?"

"I'm sorry, Mr. Seratino, but a more likely scenario is one to two years on the cadaver list. There simply aren't enough kidneys available for every patient to receive one as soon as they would like, and of course, the patients who have been waiting the longest get the first kidney available that matches."

"What! You've got to be kidding. That's ridiculous! I'm sure you can make some exception for my son. Do you know who you're talking to here? How about testing my brother and sisters, or Rosa's two sisters?"

"Emilio, my sisters are in Italy! We haven't seen them in ages. What do you want me to do, just up and ask them if they'd be a donor for our son?"

"They're family, Rosa! Hell, I know *my* brothers would donate! And what about Tim, Lorena's husband? He's probably been too busy tasting doughnuts to consider even being tested yet! Look, Doc, we'll get them in here for you. I've got lots of friends!"

"Aunts and uncles, cousins, et cetera, are all possibilities for a match. However, I might add something to help clarify things a bit. There is an upper age limit for donors as well as a lower age limit. And if Rosa has diabetes, her brothers and sisters might be diabetic as well. Just how old are your brothers and sisters? We usually don't take anyone over sixty-five."

"I'm the youngest in my family. Pascale is sixty-two and Annalisa is sixty-seven," Rosa replied quietly.

Emilio glared at her unsympathetically and said, "But I got Philippe, and he's only forty-seven. And Rollo is about that age. I should have thought of them sooner. And Tim and Sam, we'll get them in here, I promise."

"Well, it certainly looks as though you have people in mind, but you know we need to have their consent." *They also need the right genes. Emilio isn't a blood relative, so how do I tell him that?* Eric thought. "Actually, we can have them tested in their own city—have local laboratories draw their blood and send it to us."

"Fine! I'll see to it they're all called," Emilio mumbled. "Great help you are, Rosa," he continued as he reached for his coat.

The Seratinos rose and left the office with Emilio obviously upset with the whole process. They brushed past Potwin in a white lab coat. Rosa glanced at him briefly and then turned her head. Emilio was too agitated to notice anyone. He was busy mulling over in his mind how he could change the process and get his son a kidney.

Howard Potwin continued down the hallway and stepped into Eric's office.

Strong looked up and said, "Funny you should show up. Now, this wouldn't be about the Seratino family, would it? I'm guessing you had a conversation with them too. How did *that* go?"

"I have no qualms about the care you're giving Nick Seratino. It's just that Mr. Seratino called me the other day and asked that I follow along."

"Like looking over my shoulder? Following along, or steering the ship?"

"You know wealthy people expect red-carpet service."

"You can have them if you want. No one in the family matches Nick so far, and I'm afraid this family is going to be a pain in the rear."

"Even the mother doesn't match?"

"She matches, but she appears to be diabetic. Mr. Seratino is going to call the troops for cross matching—his brothers, his nephew, and even his son-in-law. For all I know, he'll probably set up a website called 'Check and see if you match Nick Seratino for a kidney.' But there's a problem. He's not the father. He's a total mismatch. I didn't think it prudent to bring up that subject, do you?"

"Sometimes we have to just baby these types of people. If we get him a match sooner, they'll be out of our hair, right? All we have to do is move him up on the transplant list. It's unlikely any patients will ever know the difference."

"You too, Howard? I can't believe this! Tuttle called earlier and wants Deaconess to make front-page news by getting Nick an early transplant. This move may gain the hospital some passing fame, but my integrity is on the line here. I don't want to make special provisions for a few select people."

"We make exceptions all the time with patients. We may move some up on the surgery schedule or may see sick patients sooner in our office when we know they need to be seen. We fit our personal friends into our schedule all the time."

"This isn't the same. This is a life and death issue for these patients, and we have to have some order and control here or it would be pandemonium."

"Just consider it. It could mean a positive image for our program to transplant a prominent citizen like the Seratino boy."

Shaking his head, he turned away from Potwin. He glared at his watch with disgust and realized he'd have to think about this later. The last surgical case was due to start soon, so he headed toward the operating room.

CHAPTER 16

The sun shined brightly through the kitchen window onto the breakfast table where Leona Ward sipped her coffee with her head bowed. It had only been a week since Mickey had passed away. Leona had made the decision to cremate his body and scatter the ashes along that fateful path that was his favorite motorcycle route and the last place he was still alive.

A tear trickled down her face as she thought, *I really miss my Mickey. He was so full of life, even if I didn't always agree with the life that he lived. I just hope his kidneys have helped someone else. I wonder if they will let me meet the persons who got Mickey's kidneys. I hope so. I just have to get myself out of this house and move on. Maybe they will let me volunteer in the dialysis unit.*

☙❧

"Adam, guess what? We have the tissue typing results back already. Things got pushed forward by Potwin and Tuttle. Now here's the shocker. The father is a total mismatch—hence, not the father. For your information, I chose to keep this quiet. I just can't tell Selena. I have no idea how she would react, but it probably wouldn't be good, and I'm not sure she's on the best terms with her father anyway. I think it's better to let a sleeping dog lie. I'm not going to tell Nick either. After all, it's more than genes that make a father. No need to make things worse with them. Besides, who knows what Mr. Seratino would do? This has really been one of those weeks hasn't it.

"Once Potwin and Tuttle, those stars of integrity, heard the news, they wanted me to bend the rules and push Nick up the list to get the transplant early. I can tell you I'm not going to do it. I can't in good conscience make this kind of exception. I have people like Derrick Jones just as worthy of needing a transplant waiting patiently. Who knows, I may be off the case if Potwin takes over, but he says that he's there just to advise for this very special person. Anyway, I'm ready to put this behind me and join you and Pam for the hospital Christmas party tonight. Selena, who didn't even want me to meet Nick or her family, now acts like his guardian angel. At least I can get Selena away from this tonight. Maybe a few drinks will put everyone at ease."

Heading back to his apartment, Eric mulled this over in his mind. *I don't know exactly how to handle Selena with this news. I just can't tell her about her father. She would be so upset. Probably best to keep this my secret.*

Even during showering he couldn't get these events out of his mind. He slipped into his tuxedo and looked at himself in the mirror. *Considering how this week has gone, I don't look too bad. Bond. James Bond. Give me that martini. Shaken, not stirred.*

Stepping into his Porsche, he gunned the engine a bit. *Feels good to let it rip around the corner,* he thought as he headed to Selena's dormitory.

Feeling somewhat cocky, he strolled to the front desk. The coeds' heads turned as he walked in. Not exactly the university dress code.

He asked the receptionist to call Selena's room. "Tell her Bond is waiting and the Aston Martin is outside."

Giggling, she did exactly as he asked. Moments later Selena came down the stairs dressed in a tightly fitted long black dress with a deeply plunging neckline that complemented her athletic body.

"Excuse me, I'm looking for Bond. We have a date tonight, and he doesn't seem to be around."

"All right, all right, I get it. He left, but now you have someone even better!"

As they drove to Cresthill Country Club for the party, they made small talk and avoided discussing Nick. Patches of snow along the roadside gave a Christmas feel to the night, and the lights on the trees sparkled.

In the clubhouse parking, few spaces were available, so Eric dropped Selena at the door and found a place for the Porsche.

Selena walked in, and Adam and Pam spotted her and introduced themselves. Eric had shown them pictures and had talked so much about her, they knew who she was.

"Wow, you look fantastic, Selena," Adam commented.

"Well, your wife looks great in that red dress, and it looks so festive."

Eric walked in and approached the threesome. "Adam, you're too damn lucky. Look at you, Pam, in this gorgeous red dress. So you've met Selena. Let's get some bubbly and hors d'oeuvres."

Tuttle stood at the entrance to the banquet room greeting everyone, and when he spotted Eric, he gave him a big smile and vigorously shook his hand. "Now who is this gorgeous woman with you, Dr. Strong?"

"This is Selena Seratino." Eric made introductions.

"Seratino, Nick's sister? We're so sorry about his condition, but we are going to do everything to get him well, right, Eric?"

"Of course we are. We want the best for all our patients."

Finding a table in the corner, they had a few glasses of merlot with the buffet meal but avoided any conversations about Nick.

"Thank goodness Potwin and Tuttle are on the opposite side of the room," Eric said. "We can avoid them as much as possible. By the way, Selena is a brilliant chemist. You may not know that she works in our laboratory on the weekends, but she is an honors graduate student at Providence. I know I only tell you about her looks, but she has brains too."

"For some reason, chemistry was not that easy for me," Pam interjected. "So I can appreciate how smart you really are."

"Don't kid yourself, Selena. Pam is a fantastic pathologist. She can come up with a diagnosis when no one else seems to know the answer."

Her scent. Her shoulder-length hair. The sway of her dress as she dances. Eric was captivated by Selena as he placed his head next to hers for their last dance together. He pressed himself into her.

After a light dessert and decaf coffee, they decided to leave. Grabbing her hand as he led her to the door, he said, "I'm sorry about your brother. I'm going to do all I can to get him a kidney, but I'm getting a lot of pressure from Howard, my partner, and Tuttle, the CEO of the hospital. Selena, you know I would do anything for you, but I can't change the rules for your brother. I have to consider all patients."

"Eric, I understand. Is my father an issue here? If he is, I'll tell him he has to get the hell off this kick. He's always trying to get his way, and quite frankly, he usually does. I'm sorry that you have to meet him this way. He means well for us, but he does have his favorite, and Nick is certainly the one."

"Just as long as you know I don't want this to come between us. I can step out of the picture and let Potwin take over."

"Never. You're the best, and don't you forget it." Her lips met his in a passionate kiss.

Eric couldn't resist giving her another kiss and letting his hands explore her body. "I'm really glad that you like my friends."

She reciprocated, pulling him closer and pushing her chest into his. "Who cares about your friends? We agreed not to talk about Nick tonight. So let's not talk about your friends either. It's you I care about."

CHAPTER 17

Dan answered as Eric called the lab.

"Hey, Dan, any news on the Seratino crossmatch yet?" Eric Strong inquired.

"The latest guy to be tested is not a match. Let's see, we have about seven negative relatives so far, but additional specimens keep rolling in."

"No one's even close?"

"Sorry to disappoint you, Eric, but nothing has shown up so far."

"I can't believe it. The two youngest dialysis patients both have families that don't match them or are sick! But it's not your fault, Dan; just keep me posted if something turns up."

Eric thought, *Crap, I'd hoped we would find someone amongst this bunch that would match so we could get this over with.*

༖

Nick's English class had its share of surprises when Nick returned to school. Two compositions were to be completed weekly, and the students were free to choose the subject matter. Nick had heard this class was a "flunk-out class," one with a reputation for eliminating the weaker students, so he tried hard to think of topics that would be unique from everyone else.

Hmm ... these guys don't know anything about dialysis. This might give me a competitive edge.

Nick didn't realize it, but college life had changed for him. Sure the frat brothers stopped in occasionally, but word of his dietary restrictions spread quickly, and the trips to the pizza parlor and local bar disappeared into thin air. Nick knew his father probably had managed to get Nick his own room at the frat house, but what had once been a playground for the nineteen-year-old now seemed more like a cell with elaborate electronic equipment replacing the human contact Nick so urgently needed. In a strange sort of way, Nick found himself having more study time than ever, even though he had to go to dialysis three times a week.

Nick completed his first composition and added a limerick on a whim at the end:

My dialysis treatment's so boring,
I'm counting the patients' loud snoring
And remembering the days
When a simple, sweet gaze
Would send all the women's hearts soaring.
Student # 542

Nick mused at his work and smiled. The idea of a limerick at the end was spur-of-the-moment, and it offered him a chance to show off some of his writing creativity. He had heard that students should try to distinguish themselves by some form of individualism, and this would be his niche. He had always been able to make people laugh, so why not give it a try in English?

(§)

Eric completed one more short surgical case before he had his afternoon office hours. He caught a quick bite in the cafeteria and then headed to his office.

He was surprised to find Howard Potwin and John Tuttle waiting for him. "Howard, Mr. Tuttle. So what do I owe this pleasure?"

"Eric, we've had a conversation with Emilio Seratino. We're going to need to reconsider how soon we can get the Seratino boy a transplant."

"So, Howard, how do you think that can change?" Eric replied with irritation. "Nick is already on our transplant list."

"The Seratinos are offering five million dollars to support our transplant program, provided Nick gets a transplant right away. Five million is a ton of money, Eric, and we all know how much this is needed for our program here at Deaconess. It would allow us to buy antirejection drugs for indigent patients as well as to purchase new equipment to transport donor kidneys."

"What does this have to do with me?" Strong replied.

"We think Nick should get the next kidney that matches him, regardless of his place on the transplant list."

"Come on, Howard, we can't be bought by an arrogant businessman who just happens to want things his way!"

"Eric, you can't blame a father for wanting to do what's best for his son. You don't have children, so you don't know what that's like," Potwin replied.

"This man knows many influential and wealthy people,

and transplanting his son will make headlines in the *Tribune*. Besides, no one but the Seratinos and us has to know, if we just keep quiet about it," Tuttle added.

"Listen, you know that there is concern that the wealthy are being recipients of transplants at higher rates than the average population, and I think it's unethical to make special concessions to one family just because they offer to give our program money."

"We wouldn't be doing anything out of the ordinary then, would we? We're talking about improving things for everyone, not just Nick! True, we would have to move down another person on the transplant list, but it's unlikely to make much difference. No one would have to ever know if we juggled the list, would they? That is, unless some new idealistic doctor gave us a lot of trouble in doing this," Tuttle said.

"We respect you, Eric, but you're young. You don't always understand how things have to go on here at the hospital. What if our program had to close? What if the Seratinos took their son elsewhere? What good would that do any of us? None, that's what! Now, instead of being so arrogant about this whole thing—obstinate might be a better word—we were hoping you'd be the type of guy who we could work with."

"Is this a threat or a joke?" Eric asked.

Tuttle said, "We're dead serious, Eric. Just keep in mind that we're the ones who hire and fire around here, and we expect results. It'd be a shame to lose you after only one year, if you get the gist of what we're saying. Not too many institutions would question a decision to hire a different doctor in the transplant program, in case that made a difference in your cooperative decision."

"Look, I'm just trying to be fair!" Eric said after a long pause. "Let me think it through a bit, okay? If this is so important, why don't the Seratinos switch doctors?"

"Emilio doesn't often switch people. He figures you'll eventually see the benefits of helping him out. Of course, we told him we operated as a *team* here at Deaconess. And we do work as a *team*, don't we, Dr. Strong?" Potwin asked.

"Team? Look, this seems more like a dictatorship. I'm sorry, gentlemen. I'm a professional, and I obey the rules."

"Think about it, Eric. We're not saying *change* the rules. We're just saying that if you ignored them this once, why, we wouldn't notice it at all. This could change your future," Potwin responded with a dour expression.

"Look, if you are wondering about publicity, how about this one? Wealthy businessman's son needs a transplant and, guess what, he's not the father."

"What are you talking about?" Tuttle asked.

"Howard knows these things happen."

"Tissue typing showed no match," Potwin stated reluctantly. "Emilio isn't the father."

"Oh my God. Well, let's not have this get out," an exasperated Tuttle responded.

⑤⑤

After he got off of the phone with Emilio, Sammy Berino thought, *So he wants me to look into this so-called tissue typing. I have no idea what he's talking about. I don't think he does either, but whatever Mr. Seratino wants, I'll try to get it for him. I'll just go for it. Tissue lab here I come.*

⑤⑤

"I just can't get ahead of these bills, and my parents have to bail me out," Kara Nichols complained to her lab tech partner at the hospital cafeteria as Sammy Berino listened intently from the adjoining table to what she was saying.

"Just about the time I get a dollar ahead, I start hearing all the advice I can hardly tolerate. You know—it's 'don't go out tonight, it just costs money.' Or 'stay away from Jake. He's trouble.'"

"Look, Kara, you're an adult. I wouldn't pay any attention to them," Jenny Coe, Kara's fellow lab worker, responded.

"I'm not going to. I've got to have a life," Kara explained as she headed toward the tissue-typing laboratory.

Sammy met her in the hallway. "So you work in tissue typing. That sounds so interesting. My employer's son is getting tested for a transplant. He just doesn't seem to get all the information from the doctors. Any chance you could help us out? Mr. Seratino would be happy to reimburse you for your time. You know, these tests are his son's tests, not somebody else's, so they really belong to him."

Sammy's request seemed so harmless—just provide him with Nick's kidney tissue type information for $200 cash. Kara obliged and used the money to pay for a car repair bill. After Nick's tissue type came more requests for those of the potential donors, and each question netted her a small amount of money.

Sammy had judged correctly in the cafeteria. Here was a girl who would be willing to bend the rules, and now it was paying off. So what was Seratino going to do with these results?

I guess he just wants a little insurance package. Having the results, he could potentially find a donor elsewhere. He's turned to the black market before.

CHAPTER 18

Nick got the English paper back with a B+ and was encouraged by the comments written on the paper. Cute, she had written. He needed some encouragement, now that his social life had come to an abrupt halt. He thought more and more about his so-called friends and realized his false ID was probably as much a liability as a benefit. At least the guys stopped into his room for it, but it was almost like a bribe for their attention.

He tossed the ID into the trash and resolved to excel at homework for a change. His next composition ended with another limerick, this time trying to show more humor:

There once was a patient named Joe
Who thought his dialysis too slow.
The nurse turned up the rate
To three thousand and eight,
And po' Joe ain't no mo!
Student #542.

Again, Nick got his paper back and felt a sense of pride

in the work he had completed. B+ again. She didn't like the ain't. *Okay, but she thought it was cute. I think if I keep this up, I can work up to an A. She seemed to like the limericks, so I'm going to write another one with my next paper.*

I wonder what the grader will do with this one.

I once was a young stud with pride,
Who toted a chick on each side.
But now the women at my bed
Are all nurses instead,
Alas! I am most dissatisfied!
Student #542.

⟨⟩

The young graduate student thumbed through her papers to grade "Mr. Limerick." She was intrigued by this student. *What could be going on with him? Nurses? Is he sick?*

⟨⟩

Potwin found Tuttle fidgeting behind his desk. "What's the problem, John?"

"Seratino called again. Always the same thing. Where's that kidney for his son? Each time he gets more threatening."

"What are we going to do?"

"John, you're not the only one he's calling. He has my number too. Unless we get Strong off the case, I don't think there is much else we can do. Why don't we tell Emilio just that? Eric won't have a say if Eric isn't his doctor, right?"

Emilio Seratino answered on the third ring. "Seratino here," he answered brashly.

"Mr. Seratino, this is Dr. Potwin. I'm here with John Tuttle. Can you hear us okay on this speaker phone?"

Emilio was amazed that they asked such a stupid question. "Yeah, I hear ya. So what's up?"

"You asked me to check in on your son, but Strong is the doctor on the case, and he's sticking with protocol. We really can't make any exceptions as long as he's his doctor. He's the physician of record and is caring for your son. You've got to convince your wife to change doctors."

"Aren't you in charge? Can't you just tell Dr. Strong to get him a transplant? Hell, I don't know what's wrong with Rosa lately. She hasn't been doing much of anything but cooking diabetic food and crying. I mentioned your name to her and she became unglued. She said we're not changing doctors, *period.*"

Tuttle looked at Potwin's stunned face. If anyone was going to speak, it would be Tuttle, so he answered slowly. "We see, Emilio. We don't want to cause trouble between you and your wife."

After he recovered, Potwin said, "I can take Strong off Nick's case. It's just that we thought it should come from you. We'll try to convince Dr. Strong to see it our way. Be patient with us, and we'll see what more we can do."

"This seems like BS to me. You tell me you're in control, yet you are wishy-washy in dealing with Strong and my son. In my business, the people listen to their boss! What is this baloney? I've got a young son whose future is dependent on a new kidney. He can't have any social life, and he spends all his time in that damn dialysis unit with old sickly people, and all you guys can say is, 'I appreciate your patience.' You've got to come up with something better than this. I'm no fool, you know!"

"Of course not, Mr. Seratino. Please believe us, we're

trying! We just wanted you to know things are going a little slower than we expected."

"You'd better speed up, or you won't be going at all!" Emilio retorted as he ended the call.

"What do you think he meant by that?" Potwin asked after hanging up. "Nick's only been a patient here a few days and just started dialysis."

"I'm not sure, but one thing I do know—his patience isn't going to last long."

෪෪

Leona Ward asked the hospital operator for the transplant surgeon on call, and Eric Strong picked up the phone.

"This is Dr. Eric Strong. What can I help you with?"

"My son, Mickey, recently passed away, and I decided to donate his kidneys. Now I would like to know if there is something I can do to help out. You know, volunteer. Maybe in the dialysis unit where those poor people are waiting for a kidney."

"Was his name Mickey Ward?"

"Yes, that's my boy. I miss him so much."

"I know exactly who he is, and I just want to tell you how sorry I am for your loss. You should be encouraged that his organs were successfully transplanted into two patients who had been waiting for a kidney for a long time. I'll bet I can find a spot for you in the dialysis center. My friend Adam Foster oversees the facility, and they can always use help."

"Do you think that I could ever meet the people who received Mickey's kidneys?"

"We usually leave this up to the recipients. They like to write letters to the donor's family expressing their gratitude and often voice the same question, wanting to meet the family as well. I will try to line that up for you through our transplant office."

CHAPTER 19

Although frustrated by the social abandonment of his frat brothers, Nick was adapting as well as could be expected for a young dialysis patient. He joked with Derrick about being the envy of the guys at campus, at least amongst the "druggies," who would have loved to have his huge arm veins. He nicknamed the patients in his dialysis bay and muttered their names whenever he saw them: Groucho for Max Strickland; Saint Evelyn for Evelyn Jones; Porky for Jess Thompson; and the Server was Tina Parker. Over the past month, Nick had tried to calm his father by kidding with him and explaining that he felt okay on dialysis, but Emilio rarely saw humor in anything.

Nick talked to his sister instead. "I know you're busy, but I've been thinking. Dad's been giving me all the attention and ignoring Mom. Dad's upset about her cooking now that she cooks with less salt and no sugar. He's mad because no one matches me for a transplant, and he sure as hell thinks Dr. Strong is against us. He calls the possibility of a two-year wait for a transplant a lousy joke. He's calling all the time giving static to this person and that, and I wish he'd cool it a bit."

"So you think this is this something new?" Selena responded. "Or is it just the first time you've noticed how things are at home. I could talk to Mom, but quite frankly, I agree with her. Dr. Strong is extremely competent and wants the best for you. You know we've been dating, so I'm pretty biased. I just feel bad you haven't been able to meet Eric on a more personal basis, but he is a great guy. I didn't take Eric's advice alone on your problems, however. You know me. I've searched the Internet and have read about all the patients waiting for a transplant, and the statistics seem staggering. The national transplant registry has set up stringent but fair guidelines for disbursement of kidneys, and though Dad may want to get you a kidney sooner, I don't see much that can be done. I'm sorry, Nick, that I couldn't give you the kidney. Life for you must be the pits."

"Just your willingness to give me a kidney means a lot to me, Selena," he said, "considering how I've treated you. I'm starting to get a new appreciation for guidelines, though. You won't believe it, but I even tossed my fake ID. Trying to be more like my big sister in my habits here! Derrick and I have been getting together between treatments, and I've even helped him at the drugstore on some of my days off. Dad thinks I'm acting like I'm slumming it, but believe me, most people wouldn't put up with what Derrick has to face on a daily basis. You've got to meet this guy. Getting to know Derrick has made this dialysis treatment manageable."

"Boy, what are they dialyzing into you? You've never talked so sensibly before."

"You're probably right. This dialysis thing does give you a whole new perspective. Listen, Selena, I've got to run. I promised Derrick I'd meet him in about fifteen minutes."

"Let's get together for a Coke."

"Sorry, can't have Coke. Too much phosphorus. Aren't you the chemistry major? Now this makes me feel good. Got one over you. How about we share a glass of wine? I can have one of those."

❁

Eric Strong arrived in the dialysis unit to check on some of his patients who may get a transplant soon. He heard Max giving the head nurse grief over the needle stick that he'd had today.

"What kind of quack personnel do we have around here?" Max complained. "She's trying to butcher my arm."

"Max, just relax. You've terrorized this young nurse enough. I'll stick your access, and we'll get on with your treatment," Nancy replied curtly, annoyed with the disruption Max had caused. "Let me try."

"All right, sweetheart. Give me a break and get the needles in." Max smiled a little too sweetly.

"There we go," Nancy exclaimed as the needle slid in. "Now settle down and finish your treatment."

"Max, the nursing staff are excellent at placing needles in the access at this dialysis center. You should feel fortunate to have them," Eric chimed in.

"Why don't you get me an access that doesn't clot and is big enough that these bimbo nurses can stick."

"Max, your access is fine. Everyone has issues from time to time with their access clotting or difficulty with the needle sticks."

❁

Nick stopped to say hello to Evelyn. "How is your treatment going today?" he asked as he stopped at her dialysis chair. Evelyn? Evelyn, what's wrong?" But Eveyln remained motionless except for twitching of her arms.

105

"Oh my God! Nurse, come quick!" a panicked Nick screamed.

"*Code! Code!*" a nurse yelled.

"Stand back, Nick. We need room here," Nancy Campion said.

Nurses from other bays raced to station twelve. Eric heard the commotion and headed immediately to Evelyn's chair. The personnel had already frantically implemented CPR with Nancy Campion giving chest percussions and Lily Thompson, the flustered nurse at the bedside, bagging the patient for ventilation. A dialysis tech called 911, and a wailing siren could soon be heard in the distance.

Nick stood behind the nurses, watching them unsuccessfully try to resuscitate Evelyn.

"Nick, you need to get out of here!" Eric yelled as the dialysis technician pulled a privacy curtain into place.

Derrick, still on the machine, cried out to the other patients, "Join me in a prayer for Evelyn."

The distraught patients joined Derrick in reciting "The Lord's Prayer."

After thirty minutes of CPR, resuscitative efforts were stopped. Evelyn's heart demonstrated no response to medication, continued chest compressions, or bagging with oxygen.

I hate this part. What caused her death? She's been doing great and was probably going to get a transplant soon. What am I going to tell her husband? Eric thought.

⚭

Robert Jones had arrived only minutes before to take his wife home from dialysis. He saw the EMS personal arrive and the panic that seemed to be occurring in the dialysis unit but was kept away by the receptionist, who told him very little.

"Mr. Jones," Eric sullenly began as he met him in the waiting room. "I'm so sorry, but I have bad news for you. While I was visiting with another patient, your wife had a cardiac arrest. We've been trying to resuscitate her for the past thirty minutes with the dialysis nurses and the EMS staff. Evelyn became unresponsive at the end of her dialysis treatment. Everyone here tried as hard as they could to bring her back, but unfortunately, we were not successful. Evelyn just passed away. I am so sorry."

Robert Jones appeared stunned as he sank into the waiting room chair. "I just can't believe it. She seemed so normal when I dropped her off this morning. If I'd had any idea she was sick, I wouldn't have left her side. I mean, we didn't expect her to live forever, but this is such a shock."

"I think it's a shock to all of us, Mr. Jones. Evelyn was such a great lady to everyone. Had she been having any symptoms at home that may have alarmed you?"

"No. None. I just wish I'd been here to tell her goodbye. The angels have her now."

"Mr. Jones, I'm so very sorry. Is there anything I can do to help? Since this was unexpected, I would like your permission to do an autopsy. It may help us discover what may have caused her death, and that information could help us in dealing with other patients."

"Whatever you want, Dr. Strong. I know she was so looking forward to getting a transplant. We've always trusted you. I'll sign any paper that would help someone else. I know Evelyn's in a better place. She always prayed the Lord would take her peacefully. She was in peace, wasn't she? She didn't die crying out or nothin'?"

"No, Mr. Jones. As far as we could tell, she didn't feel any pain. We did everything we could, and you cannot believe how sorry we are that she died."

"Died kinda peaceful?" Mr. Jones asked again. "Can I go see her now?"

The nurses lifted the lifeless frail Evelyn back into her chair as Mr. Jones tearfully said his last goodbye. The bewildered nurses tried to provide privacy and reassurance to the remaining patients as they finished their dialysis runs.

Mr. Jones signed the autopsy permit, and Eric alerted Pam Foster, the pathologist and Adam's wife, about the need for the autopsy.

"Pam, I just happened to be here today when Evelyn Jones arrested. She'd been stable, and I thought she might be getting a transplant soon. Her family has agreed to the autopsy, so it will be interesting to see what you find because there didn't seem to be any kind of warning signs."

GƆ

Eric met Nick and Derrick in the waiting room after Derrick finished his treatment.

Nick said, "Does this happen often, Dr. Strong? What a horrible experience. I've never seen anyone die before. I can't say it's like on TV. Much worse. Derrick and I prayed, and I thought he should be a minister. Evelyn was such a sweet lady. My God, wasn't that awful? I had no idea that's the way people look when they're dead. All I know is I hope I don't experience that again."

Eric shook his head. "I'm sorry you had to see this. Especially being new to dialysis—this experience can be very traumatic. Hopefully we'll find out her cause of death to reassure everyone that it had nothing to do with her dialysis."

Derrick tried to console him. "I've seen shootings on my street. When that happens, they won't let us near the crime scene. And black people don't turn gray like whites."

Shaken, that night Nick wrote a new limerick for his English paper.

Depression's a strange type of creature,
A demagogic and unforgiving teacher
Who lectures all night
That hopelessness is one's plight,
Leaving loneliness as its all-encompassing feature.
Student #542

CHAPTER 20

"Adam, any word from your wife on Evelyn Jones's autopsy ?" Eric asked.

"This is the crazy thing. Pam found atherosclerosis in her coronaries but no acute myocardial infarction. In fact, all her organs were intact, with nothing to explain her death. She's kept serum and blood samples to study this further to try and come up with an answer. Cultures are pending, but high potassium wasn't a problem because it was the end of dialysis. As you know, she did have an arrhythmia on the EKG that was recorded by EMS—ventricular tachycardia but without any acute heart damage and normal electrolytes. Just can't explain this."

I don't want to go, Nick thought as he entered the dialysis unit for his remaining treatment of the week. He stared at the station that had been occupied by Evelyn.

Evelyn was sitting right there two days ago, he thought. Although a social worker had been assigned to patients to help them deal with their fears and grief, she did little to allay those that Nick experienced.

An older woman stopped to visit him sensing he was upset. "I'm Leona Ward. I'm just helping out here. Is there anything that you need? That is, I know that you need a new kidney. I gave my son's kidneys to help people like you."

Nick was incredulous that someone could really do that, actually give her son's kidneys away. He thanked her but told her he was okay. "I'm just a little shook up over Evelyn's death.'

"I can understand that," Leona replied.

After finishing his treatment, Nick drove to Selena's dorm and invited her to a light supper. "There was this lady, Evelyn, who died during dialysis the other night. I was just across from her, and it scared me to death. I can't believe her heart just stopped. It's not that I knew her all that well, but it hits you in the face how God could take such a gentle lady and let her die. It was frightening. And here I have the same problem she had. It gives me chills just seeing her empty chair."

"You actually saw her die? How awful! Do they know if it was a heart attack or something?"

"No one knows yet. That's what's so bad about it. If they know, they aren't saying. They think she had a heart irregularity that started at the end of her treatment, but it's not clear what caused her death."

"Nick, I just hate this for you. It's so unfair that you have to go through all this. I wish I could say something to help you. It just makes me sick."

"There's not much anyone can say or do right now, Selena, but it does help having you listen. You don't know how much I appreciate you taking time to be with me."

Two weeks after Evelyn's death, Max Strickland, in an unusually happy mood, showed up dressed as Santa.

"Ho-ho-ho!" he yelled out as he wandered his way through the facility handing out small bags of candy.

"Is this Mr. Bah Humbug himself?" a nurse who often felt Max's wrath commented to a nurse sitting beside her. "Maybe we're going to see a new Max Strickland. After all, a death in a dialysis unit can affect everyone in different ways. This is a pleasant surprise to have Mr. Grumpy here saying ho-ho-ho."

Max swept through the facility, almost dancing from patient to patient, but some had to turn down his candy because they were diabetic. Completing his rounds of merriment, he headed for the door, saying to the nurses, "I hope this gives the others some holiday cheer."

Within a short time, the patient care technician who was checking on Jess Thompson noticed that he didn't seem to be himself, and she wondered if his blood sugar might be low. He never controlled his diabetes and had blood sugar numbers all over the map. Shaking him, he wasn't responding, and she noticed his hands twitching. Was he having a seizure?

She felt for a pulse but couldn't find one. She pressed the button to get a stat blood pressure measurement, but no blood pressure could be registered. Suddenly it struck her that he was coding. She yelled out for help, and nurses and techs immediately ran to that station. The receptionist called 911, and the nursing staff started CPR.

After more than thirty minutes of CPR, there was no response, and Jess was declared dead. Nancy called Eric Strong to report the death.

Eric made his way back to the dialysis unit to talk with the shaken nurse technician who found Jess and she walked him step-by-step through what transpired.

"He'd been okay when I checked on him earlier, but then he was unresponsive. No pulse. No blood pressure. Everything with dialysis seemed normal."

"It's okay, Elva. It was nothing that you did. Two patients in two weeks. This makes all of us nervous. I don't remember this ever happening before. I hope that we can find out something this time," said an exasperated Eric Strong.

🝏

"Is this Steve Thompson, the nephew of Jess Thompson?" Eric asked.

"Yeah, sure. What's going on with old Jess?"

"It's not good news. You're listed as next of kin, and unfortunately, he had a cardiac arrest and died. We are so sorry for your loss. Since you're listed as his power of attorney, I'm calling to see if you would agree to an autopsy so we can try to determine the cause of death."

"Is it going to cost me something?"

"No, you won't have to pay for it. We want to try to prevent any future problems like this. Hopefully we'll find cause of death with the autopsy."

"Okay then, no problem. Poor Jess. He never could catch a break."

🝏

On the following Monday, Nick came to his treatment and wondered why there was an eerie quietness in the unit. Even Derrick seemed subdued and sullen.

"Hey, what's wrong with you, Derrick? You look like you ran into a wall."

Derrick started the long explanation by pointing to the empty dialysis chair. "Where have you been, man? Didn't you hear about Jess? He's dead."

CHAPTER 21

Autopsy rooms are always ice cold, perhaps to control odor, perhaps to preserve the body as it is examined, or perhaps one feels chilled to the bone even if the room is adequately heated. Today was no exception. Jess Thompson lifeless body lay on the stainless steel table. It was a shame that no family members were clamoring for the autopsy results.

Eric Strong normally didn't attend autopsies, but Jess Thompson was another patient on the transplant list. This was starting to get very personal, and he wanted to witness the autopsy himself to help find a cause.

Jess was obese, and Pam needed the assistance of Jim, the proctor, to help her get Jess's body into a working position. Eric donned a gown to help out as well.

Once they had the chest cavity opened, Eric looked over Pam's shoulder to get a view of Jess's heart. He had concluded it had to be a heart attack with his large size, poorly controlled diabetes, and hypertension. However, Jess's heart did not have any pale areas to suggest heart ischemia or infarction. On the contrary, Jess's vessels were surprisingly clean.

Although there was some arteriosclerotic disease, there was no coronary thrombosis. There also was no valvular disease and no evidence of infection in the heart. Jim placed the heart tissue samples that Pam gathered in bottles of formaldehyde so they could be sectioned and examined later under the microscope by her.

"I don't get it, Pam. Nothing seems to stand out here. Surely a cardiac event would have explained this, but at least on the surface, I don't see anything that gives us an answer."

"I agree. Unbelievable! How can two people in the dialysis unit die without an obvious cause? This isn't going to be an easy one for Adam to swallow either." She again went over the organ exams and then grimly closed the surgical openings.

"Ain't never seen anythin' like this before," Jim commented. "Why, it's like somethin' out of the blue jest bit ol' Jess and he died. Lord, have mercy on his soul. He didn't have no family or such. I reckon the Lord jest thought it was his time to pass. Who's claimin' the body? Or is it the city's case? Lord, I hope they can find a suit for Jess, he probably never had one himself. I reckon you can jest say 'heart problems,' Doc. Ain't nobody goin' to question you anyhow on this one. So stop stewin' over it. We can jest close this one up quick, and I'll call the mortician to come get him."

Eric and Pam knew very well that Jim's comments were more for show than for a lack of concern. They knew Jim had provided suits for the indigent for burial purposes, but Jim's charity was a quiet one that was not done for self-recognition.

Two days later Eric couldn't wait any longer and called Pam for the results. "Tell me the slides demonstrated a really massive heart attack."

"Sorry, Eric. Nothing. I know what you're thinking. How can that be? I don't know, but nothing is showing up. I'll save the samples for later in case we can think of anything else to test. I know this is rough on you, but it's not your fault. It's probably a fluke that this happened twice in a row. Don't get down on yourself."

"You're probably right. Just keep thinking, and I'm glad you're saving samples. We may think of something later."

෬ෟ

The harsh sound of the alarm clock woke Selena at 6:30 a.m. She rolled over, groaning about having to get up. "Why did I take this job on the weekends at Deaconess?" she asked herself. "I don't need to push myself this hard."

On the other hand, Selena knew the job gave her experience in research and would help her to decide if biochemical research might be her thing. She rolled out of bed and dragged herself into the bathroom. She considered washing her coal-black hair, but time wouldn't allow it to dry before work. She grabbed her gray Providence sweatshirt that easily hid her well-proportioned physique. Her smooth, olive complexion gave away her Italian ancestry. Because she ran five to six miles three to four times a week, she didn't have an ounce of excess body fat and had a fantastic figure, as Eric knew very well. Selena spent most of her efforts on improving her appearance through natural means, not on buying the latest cosmetics. Her exercise efforts, along with the natural beauty that she inherited from her mother, made her a striking young woman.

Selena arrived at Deaconess shortly before eight o'clock, the time that she was to start work. She was assigned a desk area that another employee used during the week, but she kept notes on the projects that she was working on in the upper drawer of the desk. Lying on the desk were the instructions that the weekday employee left for her to do during the weekend. They'd been working on a special project with a group of oncologists, testing a new marker for breast cancer. The physicians at Deaconess Hospital were unique in that they had lucrative private practices, and they were also involved in clinical research as well. Selena was to evaluate various dilutions of test markers against serum of known breast cancer patients to see if any of the markers would have identified the patient's disease in advance. The study included normal controls, and the results were blinded, so Selena would not know if the patient had breast cancer or not.

As she went to the freezer to select the samples waiting for her, she noticed other serum samples sitting on the shelf in a test-tube rack. The names of Evelyn Jones and Jess Thompson sounded eerily familiar. *Wait a minute. These are the patients who died in dialysis. I wonder what they're doing here.*

Selena called out to her supervisor, "Jan, I found samples of serum in the freezer next to the blood samples I was to analyze today. They were labeled with patients' names from dialysis. Why in the world do we have them?"

"The pathologists do that quite often. Whenever there's a suspicious death, they save the serum for future testing. It's sorta like how the police department handles unsolved murders. The pathologists keep thinking something new might show up."

"You mean the pathologists think this could be a murder?"

"Heavens no! But you know how pathologists are. They all want to be able to figure out why a given person dies. Don't think any more about it, and bring over the samples you were supposed to get."

"But my brother is on dialysis, and he's talked to me about these weird deaths. It's scared him. And now everyone in the dialysis unit is on pins and needles for fear something will happen to them. Do you know anything about their cases?"

"No, but something will show up sooner or later. Don't let it bother you. They'll probably figure it out eventually. It's just two cases."

"You're probably right. I was just asking. But how long do you keep this stuff?"

"Depends on the doctor, but they can store samples quite a while. What's with all the questions, Selena?"

"Oh, nothing. I just get harebrained ideas sometimes. It would be sorta fun to see if we could find something, don't you think?"

"We can't do squat without the doctor's permission, and Dr. Pam Foster is one bright cookie. What could we do that she hasn't already thought of?"

"Probably nothing. But then again, how do we know unless we ask? I know her. Met her at the physicians Christmas party. She seems nice. Do you think that she'd mind if I called her?"

"She'd probably love it. Why? Do you have ideas?"

"Not hardly. I mean, I don't even know what's been done or tested for," Selena replied.

She returned to her desk and completed her work for the day. The supervisor was probably right. Dr. Foster was a thorough and intelligent physician, but the lure of investigating unsolved deaths brought out Selena's feisty side.

She planned to call Dr. Foster on Monday between classes. Maybe she would even meet with her and she might tell her about the autopsy results. Right now she just wanted something concrete that would help her in counseling her brother, and this might just be the thing.

I wonder if Eric could help me convince Dr. Foster to let me help.

CHAPTER 22

Selena completed her chemistry class Monday morning and had two hours before her next class. She thought she could grab a turkey wrap in the Student Union, and while there she planned to reach Dr. Pam Foster. After eating lunch, she found a quiet area from which she could make a private phone call.

"Eric, it's Selena. When I worked last weekend I found serum samples of the patients who have died in dialysis. Do you think Pam would let me do some testing of them? I thought I could talk to my professors and get some ideas."

"I'm not sure, Selena. I know you're worried about your brother, but your dad has given all of us some grief. Pam may be nervous about letting you jump into this, but you can try. Give her a call."

Selena called the hospital switchboard.

"Hold the line while I page her," came the reply.

A minute later a female voice answered the line. "Dr. Foster."

"Dr. Foster, This is Selena Seratino. I met you and Adam at the Christmas party the other night. You might remember that I'm a graduate student at Providence University. Nick, my brother, who is on dialysis, and Eric, my boyfriend, have told me about these two unexpected deaths in dialysis. To tell you the truth, it has scared our whole family. Tell me, aren't two deaths above the statistical average for this size unit? Nick told me the deaths were amongst younger, healthier patients. I work at the Deaconess laboratory on the weekends. While I was there this weekend, I noticed saved serum samples from the two patients that he mentioned. What caused these deaths, and why are you keeping the lab samples?"

Pam switched to a more formal greeting. "Miss Seratino, Eric is a bit taken with you."

Selena, blushing, responded, "I really like Eric. He's a great guy, and we've had so much fun together. I feel bad that my father has been giving him so much grief. You can say I'm taken with him as well."

"I don't think it's only your dad. His partner and the CEO of the hospital are after Eric as well. But I appreciate your concern about trying to safeguard your brother. It's professional policy not to discuss patient records without HIPAA consent. At this point, I would have no information to give you anyway. It's true that the deaths were unexpected and that we haven't yet found the cause of their deaths, but for the time being, we have to assume the deaths were normal occurrences. However, we're keeping the serum samples just in case we think of something later."

"I was thinking that maybe I could discuss possible tests with my professors at Providence. I realize this puts you in an awkward role, but if I could help you out with anything, it would be personally rewarding to me and beneficial to the rest of the patients as well. I'm not trying to act as though you hadn't done everything already," Selena quickly added, realizing that she had probably overstepped her bounds. "You checked all the usual electrolytes, I'm sure."

"Of course we did, and the tests run on those samples were not abnormal."

"Well, could have there been an allergic reaction to something that could have caused this to happen?"

"I don't know of any new products that were used in the unit, but I could ask Eric and Adam. Both have been very involved with these deaths. Actually, Miss Seratino, it's policy not to discuss these things over the phone, and I'm afraid I need to go through the proper channels before we talk any further," Pam replied.

"I certainly understand, Dr. Foster," she said, switching to a formal greeting with Pam, "but if there's any way I could help, I'd really enjoy the opportunity to get involved. I'll not be a bother to you at all."

"Let me think about it, Selena and I'll get back to you. I guess your brother is quite the comedian."

"I can well imagine!" Selena responded, smiling. "Nick has never been a stranger to anyone for long." Then Selena realized something that had not occurred to her before. Her brother had been accepted for his own contribution to society, even if it was the overlooked group of people in a dialysis unit. The thought made her grin, and she became even more determined to help.

After agreeing to meet at a future time, Selena hung up and hurried to her next class. She loved a challenge and hoped she could help Nick as well, but decided that if her father knew she was trying to get involved, he would hound her to death about everything. She smugly decided to keep this to herself.

"Adam, what's the latest with Nick Seratino?" Eric asked as they entered the hospital cafeteria.

"Nick's doing okay, but he's quieter since these two dialysis patient deaths. I think he has had a dose of maturity."

"We still have him on the transplant list, of course, but no luck so far. Speaking of luck, what do you make of these dialysis patient deaths?" Eric asked.

"Interesting you should ask. Your new honey called Pam and wants to do some outside testing on the saved serum. She wants to help Pam find a cause of death for these patients. She says it will put her brother's mind at ease if they can prove the deaths were from natural causes. I enjoyed meeting her, and you're right, she's very bright. She did say that she wanted to keep her involvement confidential. She's not even telling her family so that her brother and dad won't bug us even more."

"Boy, that family has the extremes of personality, don't they?" Eric replied. "I can tell you that Selena is great. She could probably help you, she's so damn smart. Tony Rossini told me that the dad might even have mob connections. And that comment was substantiated by Gerhardt Siller."

"Who's Siller, and how would he know?" Adam asked.

"Gerhardt Siller is president of Providence University. I mentioned to him that Emilio Seratino made a proposal to give a substantial amount of money to the transplant program at Deaconess, and Siller called me up. Siller's on the hospital board here, you know. Well, he wouldn't give details, but he insinuated that whatever Seratino wanted, we should try to accommodate him."

"Wow! A board member who calls the local physician! I'm impressed. You don't suppose it has anything to do with the mob connection, do you? Wait a minute; this mob thing is probably just hearsay. Don't go jumping to unsubstantiated conclusions, good buddy," Adam replied.

"Yeah, you're right. Hey, I've got to go," Eric said.

He headed for his afternoon clinic. Checking his schedule, he thought, *How interesting, Peter Capellino is coming in. He once was alleged to have connections to the mob in Chicago.*

Eric walked into the exam room where Peter Capellino was sitting on the table ready to be examined. He had removed his shirt and was wearing a paper gown to keep warm because the rooms were cold and sterile. The nurse had taken his vital signs and noticed he was chilling so she offered him the paper gown, which he readily accepted.

"Mr. Capellino, how have you been?"

"Couldn't be better, Doc. Thanks to you, I'm strong as a bull. But I eat too much."

"You're not alone with that, but that's a good sign. You had blood drawn earlier this week, correct?"

"You bet, Doc. You told me to get blood drawn, and I made sure that I got to the lab. Even if I woulda forgotten, the missus never lets me forget. So is everything normal?"

"It appears to be just fine. Your blood count is normal, and the CEA test, to follow up on your colon cancer, was in the normal range as well."

"So am I good enough to be a kidney donor?"

"You're a little old for that, don't you think? What makes you ask this out of the blue?"

"Well, I got a friend that I sort of owe a favor to, and he wanted me to check and see if I would match by any chance."

"This friend isn't Emilio Seratino, is it?"

"Yeah, Doc, how do you know him?"

"His son is one of my patients, and I've met the father, but I don't know him really well. Look, you've had colon cancer in the past, so there's no way you can be a donor even if you match, so just tell Mr. Seratino you can't donate a kidney."

"But you said I don't have cancer now."

"You're acting as though you want to give a kidney. But having had cancer in the past eliminates you from ever being considered a donor. Plus, you're too old, and it's too risky for you. It would be too taxing for your system at your age. That's why there are medical guidelines before you can be a donor."

"It's just that I sorta owe Emilio. See, he's pretty rich, but that was no accident. The Berino family helped him shut down a few grocery stores, if you know what I mean. And I needed a job and Emilio sorta looked after me. He made a killing by controlling the entire southside grocery business. He always gets what he wants."

"He isn't going to get a kidney from you, and that's that, understand? Peter, you'll need to be seen again in about six months. Keep eating those veggies and try to walk a little each day. The receptionist will make your appointment."

Eric escorted Peter to the exit and wished him the best. After finishing his afternoon patients, he was eager to page Adam. "I believe those stories we heard about Emilio Seratino are probably true. My patient Peter Capellino was in today, and he more or less confirmed that Emilio is connected to the mob. He apparently has used some family friend to help him in the past establish his grocery store monopoly and is even putting pressure on some of his old friends to be donors."

"Are you saying we should be fearful if his son doesn't get a transplant soon?"

"I'm not saying anything in particular, but we need to keep our eyes open. This guy is not to be trusted, and we need to be on our guard. He's not likely to stop until he gets what he wants."

"Pam and I have the weekend off, and I'm really looking forward to getting away for a few days. It will give me a bit of time to think about all this, and maybe I can come up with ideas to help you with the Seratino family. Oh, by the way, Nancy Campion asked me if it would be okay for Leona Ward to volunteer in the dialysis unit. Apparently, you had called her and I told her it was fine."

"Oh sure, now I remember. What a sweet lady. I felt so sorry for her. I didn't see any issue from an ethical standpoint. I suspect because she is very mothering, and that could help calm the patients."

"And one more thing, she asked to meet with one of the recipients of her son's kidneys."

"She had asked me the same. That's a little more problematic, but I'm sure these recipients would appreciate the opportunity. In the past, others have wanted to express their appreciation for the donation."

CHAPTER 23

Selena completed her lab and headed to visit with Professor Buxton, her professor of biochemistry. Even though she hadn't heard back from Dr. Pam Foster, she thought it would be worthwhile talking with Buxton about possible tests that could be run on the patients' serum samples.

Buxton and Selena had mutual respect for each other. Selena had earned an A in his class, and he viewed her as one of the brightest students he had ever worked with at Providence University. Integrity and hard work were becoming rare commodities in Buxton's eyes, so when Selena arranged for this private meeting, he was pleased that he was chosen as her advisor and determined to help her in every way possible.

As she entered his cluttered office, she wondered if there was anywhere to sit. He had books and journals piled everywhere in this musty and dusty environment. Coming from behind his large oak desk, he moved piles of books around to create a place for her. The light was somewhat dim, but over his desk was a large lamp shining on the piles of books and papers scattered throughout. He seemed to know where everything was located. His eyes were drawn to her as he set aside his pipe on the cluttered desk.

"Professor Buxton, I've got a great idea for a research project in conjunction with Deaconess Hospital. I haven't told you, but my brother, Nick, recently started dialysis at their unit three times a week. Over the past month two patients have died unexpectedly while on dialysis, and although both patients had autopsies, no one has been able to pinpoint their exact cause of death. I work in the lab at Deaconess, and this weekend I made an unusual discovery; the pathologists and lab personnel had saved serum samples from these patients in the laboratory freezer for use in later testing. You know what this means, don't you? It means the doctors aren't all that convinced these patients died of natural causes. So I called the lead pathologist and asked her if I could help her investigate why they died. Of all things, she is married to Nick's kidney specialist. Her name is Pam Foster, and I think she might just consider letting me help."

Buxton leaned back on his swivel wooden desk chair and smiled at Selena's spunk. "So you're going to be the great female detective that busts open the case, huh?"

"Nobody ever makes new discoveries unless they step out of the box every once in a while," an irritated Selena responded. "And I'm not guaranteed of being allowed to do a study, but I did think that having a written research proposal would help. Both patients experienced a heart irregularity, but it was my understanding that no evidence of a heart attack was found at autopsy."

"Selena, you realize I'm not a physician. I'm a chemist, and the medical issues are under the realm of doctors' responsibilities, not ours."

"I understand, Professor, but something triggered a heart

irregularity in these patients, and I want to see if a definable cause can be found. After all, dialysis deals with a lot of chemistry. You know the chemical balance in one's body, so wouldn't it make sense that there could be an electrolyte problem? It certainly would allay fears that my brother and others have about these patients' deaths."

"I'm sure the doctors have already thought of that, Selena. Besides, two deaths aren't that many considering the average age and degree of illness of these patients. Are you sure this isn't just a statistically ordinary occurrence?" Buxton observed.

Selena gave a look of disappointment.

"Let's suppose you're right and that these deaths are out of the ordinary. What do you think you could discover that the physicians haven't already thought of?"

"I don't know, sir; that's why I wanted to talk with you. Do you have any ideas on how to approach something like this?"

He thought for a moment. "Have you taken any physiology classes?"

"Only one so far."

"Did you do any experiments with animals?"

"Yes, as a matter of fact. I protested the fact that one of the dogs was ultimately sacrificed by an injection of potassium in its veins. Disgusting to have killed a dog, don't you think?"

"Better than to have killed a human, right? Besides, that's probably your answer—potassium! Minerals are important for normal heart function, and abnormalities in potassium could certainly cause heart problems."

"I believe they've already thought of that," Selena responded. "I mean, Dr. Foster told me the blood chemistry was normal for a dialysis patient."

"Then there must be something else going on. You know autopsies don't always give the cause of death. I've heard that sometimes a cause of death can never be found."

"Dr. Foster is pretty thorough, but the fact that she saved specimens indicates to me that she had doubts about the results."

"Maybe; you know her better than I do. Okay, let's consider something else. What about bacteria? After all, I believe the blood is flowing outside the body, and bacteria could potentially contaminate the system."

Selena agreed. "It's my understanding that neither patient had a fever, but that's a good thing to check on. Maybe the patients had an infection without a fever. But where would the infection have originated?"

"How about the fluid that surrounds the artificial kidney? Maybe bacteria could have infused into the blood from that fluid."

"Hey, that's a thought. But I would assume the dialyzer prevents the transfer of bacteria to the patient. What about toxins that some bacteria produce? Could these toxins pass through the dialysis fibers?"

"This is your project, not mine, Selena. It wouldn't hurt to check. What other possibilities come to mind?"

"I was thinking about the dialysate fluid again. It contains minerals and I believe sugar, but it allows the diffusion of kidney toxins out of the body. Maybe there could be a contaminant in it. Do you think that's possible?"

"You're a step ahead of me with this one, but I do think you've thought of several scenarios that should be investigated. Now that I think of it, I recall reading an article about a dialysis unit in Spain having some mysterious type of infection or manufacturing problem that caused unexplained deaths. I'll try to locate the article for you."

"Great, I'd like to see it. I plan to go with my brother to the dialysis unit this week and see how they do things. I just wanted to see if you thought the project had any merit."

Stuffing a note in his tattered briefcase, he said, "I think it should be interesting. Let's plan to meet next week." Buxton stood up to leave.

"See, it was worth my time coming in. Thanks for the help, and I'll try and write up something this week for you to review, okay?"

"Happy to help you out, Miss Seratino, but keep in mind, I'm not an expert on medical issues. I'm more geared to chemistry. Still, I'm fascinated by your ideas. Good luck, and get the proposal to me soon. Who knows? We may just be on the edge of some great adventure."

Selena smiled as she left the office. Buxton was quite a guy, but she had to settle herself down to the reality that there might be no explanation to these deaths at all.

CHAPTER 24

Nick was completing his third month on dialysis. The two deaths had been disconcerting, but now he was settling into a regular schedule of dialysis three times a week. While it wasn't great getting needle sticks and keeping tabs on his diet, he was getting accustomed to the lifestyle. His grades were remarkably better than they had been the first semester despite the time he'd had to spend in dialysis. Much to his dismay, this was a probably a result of a significantly reduced social schedule.

Despite the unwanted reason for improvement, Nick was actually beginning to enjoy studying and felt good about understanding the material he received in classes. He set new goals, including earning an A in English. He thought he was writing pretty well but decided to make an appointment with the teacher's assistant who was grading his papers to seek additional help. Although he had no idea whom this individual was, he called the English department and was able to set up an appointment for the following Tuesday.

Nick looked forward to this interaction with the assistant. He could just imagine what the person would be like, a weird little nerdish coed with her hair in a bun and horned-rimmed glasses whose whole life centered on proper grammatical syntax. Well, maybe he could charm her a little. After all, he still remembered a thing or two about handling women, even if these skills were a bit rusty.

Selena found the library on the campus of the medical school. Seeing a librarian, she asked, "Could you direct me to the section on nephrology?"

Henrietta surmised that this was another green freshman medical student. "Over there, honey—second floor. It's marked 'internal medicine.' If you want something specific from a journal, you can use these computers." She pointed to a row of PCs near her desk.

As she watched Selena leave, she thought, *Why those girls go to medical school is beyond me. They practice one to two years and then quit and have kids. I guess they just need to prove themselves.*

Selena selected about thirty articles that seemed pertinent and printed off the references. She remembered that Nick had told her that the autopsy reports had not shown signs of advanced cardiac disease, so Selena tried to avoid the articles that sounded like they dealt with this particular topic. She read the section in the nephrology text that discussed potential complications of dialysis and read about how the water systems worked in the dialysis unit itself. She thought the doctors involved surely would have ruled out the possibility of bacteria and the production of endotoxins by certain bacteria, but she made a mental note to ask Eric about this when she saw him next. After gathering the photocopied material, Selena secured her long navy coat and headed toward her apartment. If nothing else, she would be more prepared to observe things in the dialysis unit when she accompanied Nick to his next treatment.

⟨ϑ⟩

Tuesday afternoon came quickly, and Nick was eager to visit the grader of his English compositions. He had mulled over in his mind whether he should demand a better grade or just plead for special consideration. He smiled at his own plan as he thought about what his father would have done. His dad always found a way to get what he wanted, one way or another. *Hmm. Maybe I don't want to know how he gets his way.*

⟨ϑ⟩

Nick strode into the room and stopped cold in his tracks as he looked incredulously at Sandy Miller sitting behind the desk. His shocked expression was only mirrored by her obvious look of horror and disbelief.

"You. So you're Student 542?" Sandy scoffed. "I'm supposed to help the biggest jerk I've ever met in my life! Had I known it was you writing those papers, you'd have failed the class by now!"

"Sandy, I had no idea you were the teaching assistant."

"And I didn't know you were the student wanting help—or else I wouldn't have wasted my time. I'm afraid I can't help you."

"Sandy, I am so sorry about the way I treated you in the past. If there was any way I could show you that I've changed, I would." He quickly recalled their one-night stand and how he had asked her to leave ... he regretted having treated her that way, but he doubted she'd ever believe his sincerity.

"Sure, sure! It's 'Miss Miller 'to you, by the way. Do I show you to the door, or can you find it yourself? I believe it's past visiting hours in the English department."

Nick felt truly ashamed and tried to regain his composure. He realized that his past behavior was not stellar by any means and that her comments were all too hauntingly merited.

"Miss Miller, I don't blame you for being furious. You deserved better. What can I say? I can't change what happened in the past, but I'd like to have your forgiveness—and help. I need your help in English and could use help in my personal life as well."

"I don't want to talk with you about this."

"But I could use your help in writing, Miss Miller. And we could meet here in this office if that's where you'd feel most comfortable."

"I'll think about it," Sandy responded coldly.

"Well, here's my number," Nick replied, wiping beads of sweat off his forehead. "You don't know how much it would mean to me to be able to talk with you again. But what I came in for was help in composition."

Nick paused and looked pleadingly at Sandy before scribbling his phone number on a sheet of paper, placing it on her desk. Without another word, he hurried out the door, in a stupor as he left the building.

How could I have been so stupid with Sandy at the frat house?

Sandy may have been an easy target a few months ago, but now he knew he was tasting the bitter pill of justice for his past behavior. His English grade may truly have been a B, but his self-evaluation of his own conduct was hovering down near the D or F level as far as he was concerned. Life seemed pretty much worthless.

Who in her right mind would want a guy who spent twelve hours a week on dialysis anyway?

His gloomy thoughts were disrupted as the school's bell tower rang out the four o'clock chime. Hell, he had forgotten that Selena had offered to drive him to his afternoon dialysis treatment. The punctual Selena didn't tolerate tardiness, so Nick quickly headed toward her dorm.

Nick found Selena already waiting in the small reception area. She greeted him cheerily. "You're late. What took you so long? We're barely going to make it in time for your treatment."

"Sorry. I tried to get some teaching assistance, and time got away from me. We're not missing much. It's not like being late to a show or something. I can't understand what's the big deal about going with me to dialysis anyway?"

"It gives us a good chance to talk," she replied as they climbed into her BMW SUV.

Selena backed the car out of the cramped parking slot outside the dorm, and soon the two were headed the short drive toward the dialysis unit.

"How long have you been having that rattle in the back?" Nick asked.

"What rattle? Probably just a loose bolt or something."

"BMWs don't just have 'loose bolts or something.' You need to take it in and have it checked."

"Look, you'd think that for the amount of money Dad put out for this car, it'd run like a top. I told him I didn't care what type of car I got, as long as it was dependable. And what happens? I still get one that has a rattle."

"A rattle doesn't mean it's a lemon. Come on, Selena. Give Dad a break. He wants you to have something classy. I'll take it in for you in the morning if that will help you out, okay?"

Nick and Selena arrived at the dialysis unit in time for

Nick to get checked in, weighed, and have his vital signs taken.

"Mr. Seratino, how did we do on the weight today?" the nurse named Nancy asked.

"Not bad today," Nick responded, remembering a favorite book his mother had read to him when he was about four years old about a character named Nurse Nancy.

"I see you brought a friend," the nurse said with a wry grin.

"This is my sister Selena. She's going to make sure you guys toe the line caring for me," Nick responded. "Just kidding. She's concerned about me and wanted to see how we do these dialysis treatments."

"Nick has told me you're the charge nurse, Miss Campion. So tell me, what exactly goes on here?" Selena asked blandly, pretending to be a naïve visitor.

"The blood flows out of the patient's body and through the small tubules inside the artificial kidney. These tubules allow the unwanted chemicals and water to pass from the blood side to the dialysate side, thus ridding the body of the water and waste material normally eliminated by the functioning kidney."

"So how do you know how many chemicals are removed?"

"We check the patient's blood tests regularly to monitor the status of the treatment in order to assure adequate dialysis."

"Can't infections occur when blood flows outside the body?" Selena queried.

"It's an enclosed system, but sometimes the skin becomes infected where the needles are inserted. We try to minimize this from happening by cleansing the arm with an antiseptic before inserting the needles. The water system is checked regularly for bacteria, and so are the machines. If bacteria are found, the entire water loop is disinfected and retested. In some instances bacteria can produce a toxin that gets into the patient's blood. Then we may see the patient develop fever and chills, but since the bacteria itself cannot cross the dialyzer membrane, the patient's cultures remain negative."

"That's very interesting," Selena responded, making a mental note that her question about endotoxins had just been answered.

Trying to be cautious in her questions, Selena quietly asked Nancy, "Have they found any cause for the two recent deaths of the dialysis patients?"

Nancy Campion suddenly became as cold as ice. "Drs. Foster and Strong believe they died of natural causes. There is a high mortality rate among dialysis patients, you know. About ten to fifteen percent of patients die each year."

"But isn't that percentage usually among the patients who are chronically the sickest? Nick said these two seemed so healthy in comparison to other patients in the unit."

"It's policy to not discuss patients' diseases and treatments with others. It's part of patient privacy."

"Sorry, I didn't mean to put you on the spot or insinuate anything was wrong. I'm sure it must be upsetting to all of you. But do you mind if I walk around the unit? Dialysis has become a new interest of mine since Nick is on dialysis."

A guilty feeling crept over Selena as she stood up and followed Nancy Campion around the unit. The tour was exactly what she wanted, but the feeling of suspiciousness was more than she had bargained for. Patients looked at her, probably wondering who this person was. They felt on display, like a circus act. Leaving with Nick, she sensed he was upset with her.

"Did Dad put you up to this?"

"No, it was my idea. But I wanted to help you. After all,

I should have been checking on you last fall, and I did nothing but pout about your being at Providence. I just thought I could help you out now."

"Well, you can keep clear. I'll drive myself to dialysis from now on, okay?" Nick retorted as they approached his frat house. "I'm old enough to take care of myself."

CED

Four weeks passed, and things settled down in the dialysis facility. Treatments seemed uneventful, and the anxiety that surrounded the deaths subsided. Nick settled into his routine, and his fear of dialysis was dissipating. Moreover, his studies became his priority as his father continued to harass Tuttle and Potwin.

CED

Tina Parker has just finished her treatment and was walking to her dilapidated Buick, complaining as usual about her treatments. *Damn thing took so long. I need to get to work, and they're late getting me on as usual. What's with my hand? It won't stop shaking. Oh my God. My leg is shaking too. I can't walk. Someone help me. Help! Help!*

CHAPTER 25

"Adam, I just heard. Tina Parker died. I thought we were beyond these deaths. Let me guess. Nothing found again," Eric asked.

"Pam looked hard but no findings. She was off the machine and on her way to her car, so there was a delay in trying to resuscitate her. Some of the specimens saved aren't going to be very helpful, but we did keep some blood in case anything turned up."

⚇

Nick concentrated harder than ever on writing his latest English composition. His mind mulled over his chosen topic. *Dialysis*, he thought. *That's a topic no one else would write about in college. A dull topic until you live with it, a teacher that no one wants to have—but still … a lesson that has taught me so much.*

If he could just convey his insights into words, he might be able to express ideas that were fresh and new and that showed his newly attained experiences into life in general. The composition took him longer than ever, but this time he was pleased with his work. He had a feeling of accomplishment in his serious composition but couldn't resist his urge to communicate humorously once again with Sandy.

I'm wondering how to enhance
My ability to create a romance.
Should I be timid or bolder
When I face a cold shoulder
Or accept that I haven't a chance?
Student #542.

It's a long shot that she'll comment on this one, he thought, *but what do I have to lose? If there was any chance for a response, it was now or never.*

৪৪

Selena answered Pam's call. "Thank you for letting me do additional tests on the samples that you've saved. It's doubtful that I will have any better luck, but now with the third death, I'm more motivated than ever."

This third unexpected death in the dialysis unit seems to make the likelihood of coincidence an absurd possibility, Selena thought.

Pam had prefaced Selena with the warning that all their work was to be done jointly, not independently, and all findings were to remain completely confidential.

"Yes, I understand," an excited Selena responded. "Thank you so much for the opportunity to work with you. How soon can we get started on this project? I'd be available Wednesday afternoon."

"That's fine with me. Should we say at about four o'clock?"

"Perfect."

ထ

Student 542's paper was lying on top of the pile on Sandy's desk when she sat down to grade for the week. *Next semester I'll find a different job*, she thought.

Yet she couldn't resist reading Nick's paper first, scanning every sentence for even the tiniest fault. It was amazing how his journalistic style had improved throughout the semester. His insight into topics had really shown a depth of understanding and unfortunately, her desire to downgrade his paper was superseded by her desire to grade fairly. She gave the composition an A and then gave in to her desire to read his closing limerick. She was floored.

How can this guy have control over me even now? she thought. She knew it wasn't exactly professional to write a personal note on a student's paper, but she couldn't resist the opportunity. After setting the paper down and thinking for a few minutes, she wrote her response:

In peace I extend an olive branch,
But be careful how you use a second chance.
Treat women with respect!
It's something you'll not regret,
Just keep the zipper pulled up on your pants.
TA

CHAPTER 26

"I'm calling Network 10 about these deaths. This is no coincidence. In fact, I may call the police. We may be dealing with homicides," Eric said with frustration. "But who would want to knock off dialysis patients? Or is someone trying to get back at us? Since these treatments are expensive and are paid by the government, is someone trying to reduce our federal medical costs? Do you think there's any connection to the Seratino family?"

"Emilio does have mob ties, Eric, but why kill other patients?" Adam asked. "I can't imagine anybody is worried about the national debt."

"I know everyone is trying to blame the Seratino family, but give them a break. I suppose it's possible that he is trying to improve his son's chances of getting a transplant," Eric offered.

"Boy, that's a scary thought. He does seem desperate."

"Did I tell you someone hacked into the transplant database? They apparently used one of the lab's computers before the employees arrived. They aren't sure what information has been compromised, but really, the only data would be names, tissue types, and placement on the transplant list," Eric said.

"Did they try to change the positions of the patients?"

"I guess they tried but weren't successful. That requires a special password," Eric responded.

"That sounds like our friend, Seratino. Any chance Selena would have done anything? She does work in the lab and has access to the lab data system," Adam asked cautiously.

"Selena would never do that. We just had a conversation about her dad and she's as frustrated with him as anyone," Eric said.

"I know you two are very close, and she is extremely bright, but she did say she felt guilty about not paying attention to Nick during his first semester. Could she feel guilty enough to try to help him with his position on the list?"

"No way. There's no chance ... but okay, I'll keep an eye on her. I'm telling you, Selena would never do that."

☾☽

Selena arrived at Pam Foster's office shortly before four on Wednesday. Foster was reviewing slides through her microscope when Selena knocked on the door.

"Come in, Selena. Have a seat."

"Again, I just want to thank you for allowing me to be involved with this study. I'm not trying to upstage you. I just want to help my brother if I can. I won't get into family dynamics, but I've never been able to help him much until now. I promise not to undermine anything you've done."

"I appreciate that. We're not trying to protect egos; we're trying to find answers why these patients died. This is frustrating with this third death. You probably know that Eric is concerned that there could be foul play, and he and Adam may be calling the police. So we're truly working with an unknown here. I wouldn't let you come unless I had checked you out first. In other words, I've called a few of your professors at the university. The ones I reached described you as being one their most gifted students."

Selena blushed. "That's awfully nice of you to say, but I'll do everything I can to help."

"So, what do you have in mind to look into? You must have been thinking about this and have something that you want to pursue," Pam said.

"I assume the dialysis solutions have already been checked for bacterial or chemical impurities."

"Yes, they have. The dialysate solutions are checked monthly and were double-checked the day after the deaths occurred. Adam assured me that everything checked out okay."

"And were the patients on the same dialysis machine?"

"Although the patients were in the same bay when they dialyzed, they were not on the same machine. I asked my husband that same question."

"So if they were in the same area, did the same nurses take care of them?"

"It would seem likely that the same nurses delivered their care. Are you thinking it could be something the nurses did?"

"I'm not saying anything, but we want to explore every possibility, right? And the blood cultures were negative, is that correct?"

"That's correct," Pam replied, feeling as if her former medical school professors were drilling her.

"The patients had no fever before they coded, right?"

"No fever. In fact, the last patient was headed home and collapsed in the parking lot outside the building. The nurses said she had a normal temp during the run."

"How were their chemistry profiles?"

"The potassium was low at the end of each treatment, but Adam says this is normal for dialysis patients. I'm rechecking the samples from the Parker lady; she was the latest patient to die, but lab information on Tina will probably be unreliable because we have no idea how long she may have been dead before they found her. She couldn't have been dead more than an hour they're guessing, but from the ward clerk's description, Tina was definitely dead at the time she was discovered."

"And you said she died after she got off the machine? Was she in pain while on dialysis?"

"Not likely. Adam told me the whole unit would have heard about Tina's pain if she'd had any. Plus she was able to walk out to her car."

"Would the fact that she had been dead affect the lab values?"

"Yes, and certainly that will have to be taken into consideration."

"What about drug toxicology? Were any of these patients addicts?"

"I don't think so, but I'll ask Adam. Dialysis is sometimes used to remove toxic levels of medications, like in overdose cases. It seems to me that a drug level would be lower, not higher than usual after dialysis," Pam responded.

"That's logical. I was just asking. Perplexing isn't it? That healthy patients can just keel over dead."

"Very perplexing, Selena. But you must remember that these patients aren't exactly pictures of health to begin with. Kidney failure usually results from an underlying disease like advanced diabetes or hypertension. Dialysis compensates for their kidney problem, but it cannot cure their underlying disease. In most cases, dialysis is the patients' lifeline, not the patients' demise.

"So let me ask you a question. Do you think anyone would want these patients to die?" Pam asked, watching for Selena's reaction.

"You mean kill them? But why?"

"That's a good question, isn't it?"

"Are you serious?"

"Look, Selena, We have to keep all options open."

"More reason why I want to help. My brother's life is on the line here. We're going to play on the same team, okay?"

"It's a deal," Pam replied.

Eric called Selena's cell, and she answered on the first ring. "Hey, babe, how about dinner? We have a lot to talk about."

"I can't wait, Eric. Had the meeting with Pam, and I thought that it went well."

"Pick you up in ten minutes. Let's head to Lou Malnati's. I'm in the mood for pizza."

"Me too. I just got out of the shower after a run so it won't take me long."

Selena came out to his car with her hair still damp, wearing skinny jeans, heels, and a low cut blouse.

"I swear you look incredible in anything you wear. I don't know if I can concentrate on any conversation when you're dressed like that."

"I'll keep you focused, my dear. We can get unfocused later."

At the restaurant, they were fortunate to get a table quickly since this was a very popular place. Once seated, Eric ordered a pint of their beer on tap, Pantless Pale Ale, thinking, *I wish she were pantless.*

"So tell me what Pam and you talked about."

"She's as frustrated as you. She has looked hard, yet nothing really stands out. She did make some interesting comments. She asked whether I thought there could be criminal activity. What do you think?"

"I don't know, but I'm worried. These are just too many coincidences. These patients are monitored so closely; I can't imagine how someone could have done anything without it being noticed. But if anyone was responsible, we'd have to think about someone on the inside doing this since it would seem illogical anyone could just walk into the unit and secretly kill patients in broad daylight."

"Did I tell you about the day I went with Nick to dialysis? I thought just seeing the process might give me some ideas about where to start looking for a cause. Nancy Campion, the manager, was very cold and behaved very defensively. She's right there and controls everything, so if anyone needs to be considered, she would be the one."

Eric shook his head. "Adam tells me Nancy is one of the most conscientious nurses and is always concerned about her patients. She goes out of her way to check on them, even after they leave. Still, I've wondered the same thing even though Adam really dismissed this possibility. He told me he couldn't imagine her being a suspect. But I think we can't rule her out."

Selena exhaled and crossed her arms. "Has anybody considered the bio technician? After all, they repair the machines and could have modified them, which could seriously injure a patient. Who knows what changes might be made? I really didn't learn anything about the machines on my visit with Nick. Someone could have done something to the water system, but when I was walking through the dialysis unit, Nancy pointed out that the treated water is delivered to every station from a central system in the back, and this area is secured to prevent others from getting into this area. But if the central water system was attacked, it should affect all the patients."

"Wow, this is why I appreciate how smart you are. I would have never thought of the biotechnicians, but this is a very good point. The water system is a crucial area."

"I think there's a lot to consider, but right now I want to consider you. So let's eat some pizza and drink beer."

"I agree. We can think on this overnight and decide on the next steps tomorrow."

CHAPTER 27

The phone was ringing in John Tuttle's office as soon as he arrived at work.

"Tuttle, this is Emilio Seratino. I heard there's been another death in the dialysis unit and that some other patient got a transplant just last weekend. What's going on? It's bad enough waiting for a transplant, but it scares the hell out of us to see people die right next to my son and have no kidney in sight for him. Then the one kidney that comes up goes to someone else. I thought we had an understanding here."

John Tuttle hadn't heard the details about the latest transplant, but he could tell that Emilio was fired up because someone else had received the transplant that Emilio had felt was due to go to Nick.

"Mr. Seratino, without trying to sound defensive, I must ask you. Do we know if the kidney would have matched Nick?"

"Matched some lucky lady, but waiting in line has never been my style, Tuttle. And Lady Luck may just pick my son next to die like that patient did last weekend. We can't afford to wait any longer, and I've put up with your outfit about long enough."

Tuttle hung up with cold, sweaty hands. The morning newspaper had reported the latest death and had insinuated that this brought the unexpected death toll to three, a higher than expected mortality rate for the year. Now with Seratino upset, he could see the transplant program heading for disaster.

Maybe he should have access to the transplant list. After all, most people would just assume their extended waiting time was due to a failure to match. The thought of adjusting the list had merit, but where was the list stored, and who would have the entry code?

Although Tuttle didn't have the answers just yet, he was starting to develop some positive plans—at least he had an idea of what to do from here.

ᏩᏋ

Eric went to pathology once he had a break in his schedule to check on Tina's autopsy results. Dr. Bob Howard was there, so Adam had a chance to discuss the case in person with the pathologist.

"Look, Eric, there isn't much to go on here since Tina was found dead in the parking lot. We can only speculate that the cause of death was ventricular fibrillation. I was told they didn't do an EKG because it would have been flat at the time they attached the electrodes. Her coronary arteries had atherosclerosis, but I don't see any signs that would indicate an acute heart attack."

"This is the third patient that has died unexpectedly in the last few weeks, Bob. I can hardly take it. They all are on the same shift and all are younger, basically nice people, and a healthier bunch. How about the chemistry profiles? Surely something's got to show up somewhere."

"Eric, I'd look at every test in the book if it would help you out, but isn't it the best *not* to find something? You know how litigious people are these days."

"Yeah, and I'm sure Max Strickland is thinking the same thing. Max is a plaintiff lawyer on the same bay as the other three patients. He's older now, but I heard he was pretty successful in his heyday. He supposedly won a few malpractice cases against doctors, and that makes him think he's an expert at medical malpractice. Furthermore, it seems he's always hot about something. Very few patients like him, and the nurses are intimidated by his gruff behavior. Ever since his wife left him a few years ago, he feels like the whole world is out to get him, unless he gets them first."

"Just do your job well, and I don't think he'll be a threat," the pathologist responded.

"You're right. I'm most concerned about the patients' health. I can't be paranoid about a malpractice suit on top of everything else. But almost every doctor gets sued at least once during his practice. There seems to be little the doctor can do to prevent this, even if he is giving great care."

"We'll keep looking for something, Eric. I'll get with Pam soon as she finishes the other autopsies. She may have a suggestion."

⊗⊗

Selena met with her chemistry professor, Dr. Buxton, after classes were over for the day.

"Our research proposal has been accepted, but there's bad news. Another death occurred last Friday. And Eric, my boyfriend, the transplant surgeon, has brought up something very disturbing. What if these deaths are intentional? What if these are murders?"

"Who would murder the sickest patients in society? Some weirdo who wants to save the government money? Come on, murder just doesn't seem likely here."

"True, but statistics don't lie. Something weird is going on, and you can't deny the facts."

"If that's the case, we're going to have to really hurry. If these are murders, maybe your brother isn't safe after all. Whoever is doing this would have to have access to the patients and would have to be familiar with substances that would not ordinarily show up in lab screening after their deaths. We still have to consider such things as water contamination or illicit drug use."

"It wouldn't be too difficult to check for heavy metal contamination of the water," Selena commented.

"True, but one would think that the water system in dialysis would have prevented this. I found an article about aluminum intoxication in dialysis. I guess this happened several years ago when aluminum hydroxide was used to lower patients' blood phosphorus. Some patients became aluminum intoxicated. They developed brain disorders and fractures and ultimately died."

"Sounds like my professor has been doing some homework," Selena said as she pulled up a chair for some serious planning. "But it sounds like it was a long-term buildup of a drug to me."

"You're probably right about that. But you caught my interest the other day, and this old dog wanted to show he knew some new tricks too. I also looked up that Spanish dialysis unit catastrophe I mentioned when we first met. Seems a sterilant caused the dialyzer fibers to erode. Filaments broke off and caused lung infarcts or scars. Not a likely thing here, but you never know."

Selena had a lot of leads to follow, but the more she thought about it, a recurring, horrid thought crossed her mind. Could her father have anything to do with this? After all, she'd heard stories from the past that chilled her to the bone. But it made no sense to murder poor sick people who offered no financial gain whatsoever to her family.

I'm not about to let anything stand in my way. I'm going to get to the bottom of this. No matter what I find, I'm going to expose it. She left the chemistry building with a new sense of determination.

Calling Eric, she explained that she'd had her meeting with Buxton.

"I'm excited, Eric, because Professor Buxton seems to be really getting into this with me. He has brought up several good possibilities, but in the end, we tended to dismiss them all—that is, all except foul play. This continues to be a lingering possibility. But what should we do next."

"It may be time to call the police," Eric said sullenly but with conviction.

CHAPTER 28

Emilio made it a habit not to call Sammy from the house phone, so he headed out for coffee at his favorite neighborhood coffee shop, He had gotten to like Starbucks coffee and there was a small store within walking distance from home. He found that he could sneak away to this place and grab a black coffee plus use their Wi-Fi if needed.

Like all coffee shops, there were several small tables, some situated more remotely, which gave Emilio privacy to make his calls. He found the perfect place near a window, far enough removed from the cashiers and listening distance from other customers.

"Yeah, Emilio? Sammy here."

"You idiot! You don't say our names when you answer the phone!" Emilio growled.

"Fat bit of difference it makes; we all got caller ID."

"Never mind, just tell me, are we making any progress on Nick's kidney?"

"You think I'm going to tell you anything over the phone? Have I ever let you down, Emilio? We ain't supposed to be talkin' like this, remember? But yeah, I'm coming along just fine. I just don't want this to be traced back to you, you understand?"

"Sure, but it's just taking so damn long. That's all. Let me know when something turns up."

"Sure thing, boss."

The phone rang at the Seratino household, and Rosa caught it just before the answering machine picked up. She had raced from the laundry room and was out of breath when she answered with a rather loud, "Hello?"

"Rosa, I'm glad I reached you. Are you alone?"

"Yes, I am, but why are you calling? What if someone else had picked up the phone?"

"I would have claimed to have dialed wrong. How are things with Nick?"

"You should know better than I. He's okay, adjusting to dialysis fine, doing better at school, all that stuff, but this isn't the life for a nineteen-year-old kid. I don't know how long he can keep this up. It's like treading water. We're not getting anywhere, but we're not going under, either. It's Emilio I'm worried about. Emilio's been beside himself trying to get Nick a transplant."

"Emilio's still the focus, I see. Well, I'm doing all I can to make sure the transplant happens sooner than usual."

"You think you deserve a feather in your hat for some feeble effort? At least Emilio is trying to get something done. Have you been tested to see if you match?"

"Rosa! How would it look if I matched?"

"In my estimation, it'd be a whole lot better than whatever it is you're doing now. We could face that problem once you get tested."

"Rosa, you know I can't do that. It'd put us both in an awkward position."

"To tell the truth, you've never shown any interest in Nick before now, and now that he's sick, you're acting like a pompous ass who belittles my husband and calls to calm me down while sitting in an ivory tower doing nothing. There have been these unexplained deaths in the unit, and Nick is worried he'll be next. You're not connected to that?"

"Are you kidding? Of course not! I know about these deaths, Rosa, and I don't think Nick has anything to worry about. That's what I called to tell you. I wanted you to rest easier about the whole thing. You know it wouldn't be possible to show interest in Nick without putting us both at risk."

"Don't call back unless you can report some real progress. You're taking a chance to just call on a whim." Rosa hung up.

CHAPTER 29

Selena headed to the hospital laboratory for her weekend research job. For once it wasn't so difficult getting up on a Saturday morning and going into work. She was motivated more than ever to begin compiling data on the serum samples of the dead patients. She pulled several pages of notes out of her folder that she had taken at the time of her meeting with Dr. Buxton and developed a spreadsheet for each of the deceased dialysis patients.

Selena was focused and energetic this morning. Even when a coworker passed her and said, "Good morning," she barely acknowledged her but instead began recording all the lab data obtained at the time of the codes. Since the laboratory tests were done in the hospital lab, the data was on the hospital servers, and the terminal in the laboratory allowed access.

Selena took out a tablet and created columns to record the sodium, potassium, chloride, carbon dioxide content, hemoglobin, hematocrit, and white blood cell count. Separate columns for cultures were created, identifying each of the cultures with a subtitle such as blood culture and dialysate culture. She added another to identify the nurses and dialysis technicians caring for the patient and the time of death. She thought this would be helpful to identify patients who dialyzed on the same machine of the patients who had died. She considered how best to conserve the samples of serum and dialysate so as not to waste the serum yet analyze them for appropriate tests. Concluding that it wasn't necessary to repeat all the chemistry values, she picked only selected items. She knew postmortem chemistry and blood samples obtained during the code might show high potassium values, and the actual results may need to be discounted.

As Selena filled in the spreadsheet, she observed a curious finding. Potassium values during the codes were high as expected, but chloride values were also high, as was the carbon dioxide content representing bicarbonate. She decided to ask Eric about the results. She carefully pipetted a small amount of serum into appropriate test tubes to retest the chemistry values and then swabbed a small amount of sample on culture plates, marking the tubes and plates with the patients' initials and hospital numbers. She then placed a call to the dialysis facility, only to have Nancy Campion answer the phone and become cold and unpleasant once she recognized Selena's voice.

"Miss Campion, who was taking care of the patients when the unexplained deaths occurred?" Selena asked.

"I was in charge," Nancy Campion replied dryly. "But I never work alone. There were a lot of people around."

"Who were the technicians?"

"What business is that of yours, Miss Seratino? I don't think I'm authorized to give out such information to just anyone who asks. Ask your brother, for Pete's sake! I'm too busy to just chitchat about patients with someone who should be minding her own business."

Selena was taken back by Nancy's cold responses but became more convinced that Nancy actually had something to hide. But just how far could she go without putting her own brother at risk?

☙❧

Nick arrived at his next dialysis treatment whistling, grinning with new enthusiasm for his English class. *She has extended an olive branch. Maybe I can work things out with her after all. She is really cute, and I like that feistiness.* Writing during dialysis also allowed the time to pass quickly, so he asked Nancy for paper and pen, which she somewhat coldly provided.

I wonder what her problem is today.

He managed to get a lap table so he could write and even though there was a constant noise in the dialysis center, he could tune this out and focus on his writing. From time to time he stopped to think of Sandy and how he should reach out to her since she seemed to make that offer. Nick had managed to get Sandy's unlisted number from one of her old sorority sisters that he knew. He smiled, realizing an unlisted number may have been one of the reasons guys hadn't called her much before this.

Sandy answered after just two rings.

"Sandy, this is Nick. I just wanted you to know how sorry I am for what I've done in the past. I liked your limerick. It was great, and I see that you like writing these cute poems as well, but I also got the message. Believe me, I heard it loud and clear. I called to see if maybe we could get together at the Student Union for lunch at noon?"

There was a long pause before he heard her response. Anticipating that she would say no, he was delighted that she agreed to see him on Wednesday, but then he realized that was his dialysis day.

"Ohhh, Wednesday would be great, but there's one problem. I dialyze on Wednesdays, so it would have to be later in the day. So will tomorrow work? Fantastic, let's meet at the Student Union at 12:30."

Nick could hardly believe his good fortune. Smiling, he turned to Derrick. "Dude, this is going to be a good day. Date tomorrow!"

A young man who was unfamiliar to Nick was walking through the dialysis unit talking to patients. It soon became apparent he was there to encourage them about transplantation, and when asked about his "puffy" face, he explained it was from the steroids he was taking to prevent transplant rejection.

Nick thought, *Am I going to look like this?*

Max looked up from his station. "Who'd you get the kidney from?" he scowled. "That Ward boy?"

The young man was taken aback by the comment but simply replied that he didn't know the donor.

Max replied, "Let me tell you a little secret. It was the Ward boy. That kidney was supposed to be mine! I think I was on the list longer than you. Well, Nick over there is probably going to need a transplant quick. He probably can't get it up, and he's got a date tomorrow. Can you get it up, boy?"

Nick was ticked off that Max would say such a thing in front of everyone, but before Nick could say anything, Max continued.

"Hell, that's a problem all these men have. It's not just you, Nick."

Nick was furious that Max would point to him with these comments, and he wanted to just get out of his chair and punch Max in the face. Unfortunately, what Max had said was true. He had noticed that erections were rare, but he had been too embarrassed to mention this to anyone. His lack of a response went unnoticed, but the young transplant patient, hearing Max's comments, assured Nick that this would get better with transplantation. Nick was embarrassed that his secret was common knowledge among other dialysis patients, but at the same time he felt a sense of relief that he wasn't the only one with this problem and that a transplant would fix it.

"Listen, Max, we're sick of your comments! If you can't say something pleasant, why don't you keep your opinions to yourself?" Nick shouted.

"But that kidney was mine!" Max yelled once more. "I got screwed!"

A technician moved Max to a corner of the unit out of earshot of the other patients.

Selena paged Dr. Pam Foster through the hospital operator. After a few minutes, Pam answered.

Selena said, "I wanted to visit with you for a moment about the tests I completed last Saturday in the lab. Do you have time to talk?"

"Sure. What do you have?"

"I took mini samples of serum to conserve them and retested the electrolytes on the patients, and as before, there didn't seem to be any unexpected levels of potassium, which I knew could have been an issue. But there was low sodium, high chloride, and high bicarbonate. I was thinking I could explain the high bicarbonate because dialysis was just completed and that would have brought the level up, but it seems hard to explain the low sodium and high chloride."

"Interesting." Pam thought for a few moments. "So there was a low anion gap."

"Low anion gap?"

"Yes, anion gap refers to a gap between the positively charge ions like sodium and negatively charged ions like chloride and bicarbonate recorded as the CO_2 content on the electrolyte panel. This gap normally is eight to sixteen. It sounds like the anion gap in these patients may be low. In kidney failure, the gap can be high but would be partially corrected by dialysis."

"So what could have caused a low anion gap?"

"I don't know for sure, so we'll have to think this through carefully. Low anion gaps are not found often, so I'll have to give this some thought." She hung up.

Selena thought for a moment as well. *Low anion gap. I have no idea what that really means. I've got to talk with Eric. I'm sure he can help me.*

CHAPTER 30

Nick entered the Student Union late and found Sandy in a booth with a scowl on her face.

"Hey, what's a great lady like you doing crouched into the corner here? You're lucky I found you. I'm sorry I'm late. With school, dialysis, and everything else going on, it requires a master's degree in time management."

"You're the lucky one, Nick. I just about didn't come. You understand this is strictly business."

"Absolutely. Never thought of anything else. I brought along the paper I've been working on."

She said, "So tell me, what's your latest paper about, and how can I help you? Would you like a drink first? It is lunchtime, you know."

"Go ahead and get something. I'm on fluid restriction," Nick responded. Actually, he could have had a Sprite, but he felt it was in his best interest to get a little sympathy from this lady. He flagged down a waitress and ordered Sandy an iced tea.

"I'll just sit here and watch you drink while we discuss 'Ode to a Toad on a Dusty Road.'"

That made her break out laughing, but then she asked, "Is it depressing having to rely on a machine all the time?"

"You mean dialysis? Hey, people give dialysis a bad rap. It's really not so bad once you sit down and look at it. Besides, I hope to get a transplant soon, and then I'll be pretty much back to normal."

Nick handed over his current paper, and Sandy examined it. There were a few grammatical errors here and there, but the content was solid, original, and engaging.

"Hmm, very good," Sandy mused. "You're able to capture a feeling of fear, hope, frustration, and joy in a very short period of time."

"Just writing things that I've experienced firsthand," Nick responded.

Sandy continued reading until she came to the limerick.

Oh, for my past life I'm yearning,
Unwanted, the lessons I'm learning!
But dialysis, my teacher,
Is an unforgiving, cruel preacher—
I'm not living my life, just enduring.

"Nick, is this true? Are you really just enduring your life?" Sandy asked.

"We're here to talk about English, Miss Miller."

"Your formality is killing me, Nick! I'm Sandy! Are you really just enduring your life? Answer me!"

Nick rose to leave. "I'm not here to discuss my problems, especially with you, Sandy. I'm trying my best to impress you. Can't you see that? And believe me, I'm working from a huge disadvantage, considering my past. I'd just love to run away from it all, but I can't. It's like, whom am I going to talk to? My dad is all over town trying to dig up a kidney for his poor little boy. My brilliant sister is hunting down the dialysis nurses like they're some sort of murderers or something. My friends shun me like I've got the plague, and my English teacher is afraid I'm going to humiliate her again. All this, and on top of that, I've seen patients next to me die. I can't go drinking with the guys because of fluid restrictions, and three days a week, I'm tied up to a machine where the only women wanting to talk to me are about seventy years old! And I just blew my one chance to impress someone I cared about by telling you all this!"

"Nick, don't leave!" Sandy begged as she sprang from the booth and brushed by one of her old friends. She ignored the glare the girl gave her and would have punched her if the time allowed such an action. But Sandy was on the chase and no longer cared who saw her or what they said.

"Your paper, your paper sounds great, Nick. Just a few sentences here and there. Not much. I want to work on it with you, okay?"

Nick turned and stopped in his tracks. "'Just a few sentences here and there' isn't a complete sentence, Sandy. Maybe I can help you with your grammar."

CHAPTER 31

"Eric, I think I may have found something on the patients that may give us a clue to their cause of death. I called Pam, and she couldn't explain the findings. So what does a low anion gap mean?"

"Wow, Selena, you're pushing me back to laboratory chemistry. You realize I'm a surgeon, not an internist."

"But you're so damn smart, I know you know everything."

"I appreciate your confidence in me, but I have to think for a moment. Let's see, anions are negatively charged, and cations are positively charged. What were the numbers again?"

"The sodium was 130meq/l, chloride 110meq/l, and the bicarbonate 30meq/l."

"That wasn't only a low anion gap, that was a negative ion gap. Hey, I've got a lab chemistry book here in my office, so hold on and let me look. Ah, here it is, low anion gap. It says that it could be a lab error, but this would seem to be unlikely if you saw this in every patient. Very low albumin, a monoclonal IgG gammopathy, but that's seen in patients with bone marrow cancer, and none of these patients had that condition. Ingestion of a bromide like bromo-seltzer that was used years ago. No one today uses that. A high calcium or magnesium, but Pam had already checked those, right? It can be from ingestion of some drugs."

"Drugs. Hmm, let me look into that," Selena responded with curiosity.

෴

"Smooth, smooth, smo-o-o-o-oth!" Derrick exclaimed to Nick at his next treatment. "Always keep the girl on the defensive!"

"I wasn't exactly trying to put Sandy on the defense, Derrick. I was just so frustrated at having nothing go my way!"

"But she's still talking to ya, isn't she? I mean, aren't you two going to meet up again this week, buddy?"

"Yeah, yeah, later tonight for that matter, but that doesn't mean anything. She just wants to help me with my English paper."

"Knocked over a chair just chasin' you to help with an English paper, you said? Doesn't sound to me that she's just interested in your grade!" Derrick responded.

Nick knew Derrick was right and couldn't keep his smile to himself. "Hey, why have you been running late to all these dialysis treatments lately? You don't have a girl on the string, do you?"

"Man, I wish. But no, you know how it is. Barney's been short on help lately, and I just haven't gotten out on time. That's all."

"Makes the whole shift of nurses here work late, doesn't it?" Nick responded, immediately feeling guilty that he had implied that Derrick was inconveniencing the whole staff.

"Yeah, you're right. I'm going to try and do better.

Actually, I had a bit of car trouble tonight, so I walked here. But hey, got nothin' to do after this run, not like you, Romeo."

Nick laughed and patted his friend on the head as he began to leave. "See ya later, Derrick." Before leaving, he heard Max cry out from the corner of the dialysis unit.

"Get me a container or something, I'm feeling sick," Max complained. It seemed the emesis basin that was a routine fixture at every patient's bedside was missing, so Nancy rushed to the nurse's station and grabbed some supplies. She then headed back to Max and eased him back into his chair. She stayed with him for about four or five minutes before he seemed to regain his strength and insisted on heading home. His pulse and vital signs were normal, so Nancy cautiously watched him as he made his way out the door and to his car.

Nick turned once more before leaving and saw Derrick shaking all over and not responding. He screamed out, "Derrick, he's shaking and looks sick!"

"Call a *code*!" Nancy yelled to the nurses in the unit as she lowered Derrick onto the floor.

"My God, not Derrick!" cried the RN from the bay next to Nancy's. He immediately ran to Derrick's station and began administering CPR.

Nick was horrified watching the events unfold. Nancy knelt beside him with a syringe in her hand. The EMS personal arrived, and she quickly put the syringe in her pocket and called out. "Over here."

They adeptly inserted a breathing tube and ventilated for him. He received two defibrillating shocks and soon had a pulse, so they began to transport him to the hospital.

Thank God Derrick has a heartbeat, Nick thought as he glanced at the cardiac monitor.

Nick said a frantic, earnest prayer for Derrick, wondering how this could have happened to his best friend. *Derrick was fine as I was leaving,* he remembered, *but now he's motion-less on the cot.*

"Nick! What are you doing here?" Nancy cried as she watched Derrick being loaded into the ambulance. "I thought you would be gone by now."

"I saw what happened. Where are they taking Derrick?"

"Deaconess! Just pray he makes it!"

"I will, believe me," replied Nick.

He was already headed to his car to follow Derrick to the emergency room. He called Sandy on his cell phone en route to cancel the meeting they had planned for later that night. Then he called Selena for some support and had to leave her a voice mail but told her not to tell their parents. No use getting them upset about something over which they had no control. He just hoped he wasn't headed for the worst bit of news in his life.

CHAPTER 32

John Tuttle had just finished missing the ball at his racquetball match and blamed it on the beeps emitting from his hospital pager. "Damn pager!" he blasted as though the infrequent page accounted for his inept swing.

"Tuttle here," he barked into his cell phone, clearly irritated at the interruption from the nursing supervisor.

"Mr. Tuttle, we have a reporter here from the KLMW news team asking about the latest dialysis unit problem. I guess there was another patient who arrested on dialysis but survived and is in our ICU now. Dr. Eric Strong was going to see the patient, a young black kid, I didn't catch the name."

"Damn, another arrest," Tuttle said under his breath— *and the news reporters know about it already!* "Just put him off. Don't say anything to him," Tuttle instructed, wiping the beads of sweat off his balding wet head. "Just tell him it's not hospital policy to talk to anyone until we notify the family or something like that. I'll try to get up there as soon as I can. Does it look like the kid is going to make it?"

"They've got him intubated and on the ventilator but it's still pretty much touch and go."

"Thanks, Anita, I'll be up as soon as I can. You caught me on the courts again," Tuttle added, hoping to imply that this athletic outing was a routine occurrence. Although Tuttle verbalized concern for physical fitness, his rotund body portrayed a different story. Tuttle turned off the cell phone and set his racquet next to his duffel bag.

Turning to his racquetball partner, he said, "Looks like this match is over for tonight. I've got to head into the hospital, so I'll save you from an embarrassing defeat. It looks like the damn media has been doing some ambulance chasing again. Anyway, there's been another problem in the dialysis unit, and I've got to go straighten things out."

Tuttle headed to the locker room with an air of importance. While Eric was busy handling Derrick's case, John Tuttle focused on deciding which suit would best to portray him as commander-in-chief of Deaconess Medical Center. Although he feigned disgust at the phone call, he actually enjoyed the opportunity to display his corporate authority.

He grabbed his briefcase and put in a few miscellaneous papers to give a proper businesslike impression. No one would ever check the contents of these papers, but their mere presence gave an air of organization and authority.

Tuttle paged Strong, but Eric was in no mood to discuss the media concerns that Tuttle had placed as his priority and ended the conversation abruptly.

"No, I won't give a joint news conference with you, John," Eric said, exasperated. "I can't be in two places at one time. The media is your problem, and patient care is mine. This patient is still alive, and he's my number-one priority right now, not public curiosity."

"How's he doing? Is he going to make it?" Tuttle asked.

"He's on the respirator and is having some tremors and

cardiac irregularities, but I think he'll survive. We're giving it our best shot. I do think we'll have to close the dialysis unit temporarily until we figure out what's causing these recurring problems. We'll have to juggle time slots, but I think we can dialyze the outpatients in the acute area and possibly in other units here in town until we take care of this problem. Adam can manage that issue."

"Great! How's that going to sound?" Tuttle responded and then added, "And keep that kid alive, understand? There's a lot at stake here!" as though the reason for keeping Derrick alive was to maintain a pristine hospital image.

"Look, John, we're doing our best. But that's the case with every patient I see."

Eric ordered a lidocaine drip to control the bouts of ventricular tachycardia that Derrick was experiencing. He also ordered the typical blood drug screens, chemistry profiles, and blood cultures and was specifically going to look carefully at the anion gap. The results of the chemistry profiles came back quickly. Not surprisingly, the anion gap was again low so he dialed Selena to let her know.

"Eric, check lactate levels, ketoacids, and salicylate levels. And throw in a check for ethylene glycol too. I know these substances tend to raise the anion gap, but these are substances that could have been added to the dialysate. Can we check the bromide level?" Selena responded when she received Eric's call. "My brother left me this frantic call about Derrick. That's his best friend, and this is devastating to Nick. I just hope he survives."

"I'll see if we can check for bromide, and I'll test for oxalic acid and formic acid as well. That's what one expects from ethylene glycol and methanol. This time we have a better idea of what's going on. I've asked Adam to dialyze Derrick again to see if we can't get the anion gap closer to normal. We can't have another patient die, and we're lucky Derrick survived the code."

C",D

Nick arrived at the ICU waiting room only minutes before Selena rushed into the small area.

"Nick, have you heard how Derrick is doing? I'm glad you're here for him. Has anyone else in his family been notified? You must be going through hell! I just can't believe it! Have you talked to anyone about his condition yet?"

"No, I haven't yet, but thanks for being here. Who knows what's going on with Derrick—he wasn't moving when I saw him loaded into the ambulance at the dialysis unit. I just got here myself a few minutes ago."

"You mean he arrested? Who was taking care of him?'

"Nancy Campion—just like always."

"That figures—Nurse Campion!" Selena scoffed. "I've had about enough of her! What happened? Were you there when he coded?"

"I was ready to leave the dialysis unit but glanced back at Derrick. I remembered him saying his car broke down, so I was thinking that I could give him a ride home. That's when I turned back to look at Derrick and saw him jerking like all the other patients who died. The nurses were frantically trying to resuscitate him, and Miss Campion was bent over Derrick. The nurse in the other bay had already called for the ambulance. I wouldn't have left him if I had had any idea this would have happened. I feel so terrible; I just can't believe this could have happened to my best friend!"

"It's not your fault, Nick! Derrick's coding wasn't because of you. But is there more?"

"Max had just left, but when I looked back into the unit,

Derrick was on the floor, and Miss Campion ..." Nick buried his head in his arms and started sobbing uncontrollably.

"What, Nick! You've got to tell me what you saw! You aren't trying to say Miss Campion did something, are you?"

"Miss Campion had a syringe in her hand. I saw it! Ahhhgh! I can't believe it. It all fits now! Max always says Miss Campion is worthless! I don't know why I didn't jump on her when I saw it! I'm sure she had just given Derrick a shot of something. We've got to tell somebody, Selena! You know Dr. Foster's wife; tell her or Eric. Tell them now! It could save Derrick's life, and he's the best friend I've got!"

Instead of calming Nick down, Selena caused Nick to become more hysterical with fear, and he was distraught beyond control. She became more convinced that Nancy Campion was the cause of the mysterious deaths in the unit and went to the ICU entrance to try to talk with Eric.

"My name is Selena Seratino," she announced through the intercom at the entrance to the ICU, "and I'm a friend of Derrick's and Dr. Strong. Can I come in to talk with Dr. Strong?"

"I'm sorry, but only family members are allowed in to the see the patients."

"Okay, but if Dr. Strong is there, could you tell him Selena is in the waiting room?"

"He's busy right now, but I'll tell him," the receptionist added.

Within moments Eric came to the waiting room and found Nick and Selena in the corner.

"So you already heard. Well, he's alive. That's more than we can say for the others. The twitching is less, and like the others, he has a negative anion gap. He's going to get additional dialysis soon."

"Nick was in the dialysis unit and witnessed what

happened. We thought you should know something. Nancy Campion gave Derrick an IV drug at the end of the dialysis treatment. Nick saw that she had a syringe in her hand when he looked back at Derrick as he was going into the waiting room, and he saw her place a syringe back into her pocket. I've told you this lady is a witch and has something to hide."

"Selena, I don't know. Everyone else talks so positively about Nancy Campion being a great nurse. They all say she would never do anything like that," Eric retorted when he heard Selena's accusation.

"My brother saw her give something to Derrick, and he coded right at that moment. How can you deny that?"

"I can't, and we need to find out what she gave him. Regarding Derrick, he's alive and on the respirator, but we won't know how alert he'll be until he regains consciousness."

"Nick called me right away, and I came right up."

"Just hush up the rumors until we confirm what's happened. This may be the time to bring in the police. One thing I will say in Nancy's defense: I just finished talking with her on the phone. She's upset about all this too. She told me she was not going to have another patient die in dialysis on her shift."

"That's more reassuring, but I still don't trust her," Selena answered. "Have you gathered plenty of samples that we can study?"

"Yes, I drew blood samples of everything I could think of and saved more for you, my dear, so get to it."

"Aye, aye, Doctor," Selena replied as she gave Eric a mock salute.

At that moment the head nurse came out to retrieve Eric from the waiting room. "Dr. Strong, we have some more results from Derrick's lab tests."

CHAPTER 33

John Tuttle decided to meet with the reporters in a more secluded room in the hospital. He announced that the dialysis unit was temporarily closing as a precaution. The patients would be dialyzing in the hospital dialysis center until all of the equipment in the chronic dialysis unit could be thoroughly examined and inspected. He told the reporters that there still was no known explanation for the recent deaths but that the latest patient had survived the event and that the doctors were doing everything in their power to keep this patient alive. The hospital's main concern remained the well being of all the dialysis patients, who trusted and relied on dialysis three times a week for the remainder of their lives. Tuttle expressed confidence that any problems would soon be discovered and remedied and that the hospital would continue its tradition of excellent patient care that had been established over the past several years.

After the conference, Tuttle headed to his office, only to be faced with blinking messages on his business phone recorder. Tuttle easily recognized Emilio Seratino's voice.

"Get my son out of that death trap of a dialysis unit! We've waited long enough with him on that damn machine!"

Tuttle viewed the message as either a threat or a clue. *Seratino wouldn't be behind these deaths, would he?* he wondered. He remembered hearing of Mafia connections with the Seratino family, but such a possibility seemed remote. He decided instead to focus his attention on solving the immediate problem of dialyzing the remaining patients. He paged the director of nursing and discussed the details of temporarily closing the outpatient unit.

Reaching her voice mail, he decided to leave a message. "Mary, this is John Tuttle, and I'm afraid we're going to need to shut down the outpatient dialysis unit. They will dialyze in the hospital dialysis center in the meantime. We need to figure out why we're having these unexpected deaths to assure we can dialyze these patients safely. You'll need to have the staff notify the patients and tell the personnel not to come to the outpatient location before their runs tomorrow. I'm sorry about this, and you can well assume that I will be in close contact with you about this whole issue. But that is what the administration feels will be the best policy."

෨෪

Selena found Eric sitting at the physician's desk scrutinizing the recently returned lab results. "Lactate levels were zero. White blood cell count was slightly elevated—probably a result of the stress of the code. Cardiac enzymes and troponin I levels were normal, with no sign of myocardial infarction. Electrolytes testing showed that the potassium was normal, chloride level was high, carbon dioxide content high. Again there was a low anion gap—this is now the third patient with a low and negative anion gap. I have to say I don't remember ever having seen a lab result like this," Eric said.

"Has the drug screen returned?" Selena asked.

"It just came back, and there were no illicit drugs."

"What about methanol or ethylene glycol?"

"Zero. No sign of windshield washer fluid or antifreeze either if that's what you mean," Eric replied teasingly.

"It's now time for the chemistry major to take over," Selena said jokingly. "I think I'm going to consider gas chromatography. This machine will check for heavy metals that might have been added to the dialysate and given to the patient intentionally. You look a mess! You must have gotten as much sleep as I did last night. Were you on call?"

Eric replied with exhaustion, "All right, Einstein, let's see what you find out. I've got confidence you're going to turn something up. I doubt you'll leave a single rock unturned until you find the answer."

෧෮

Although Selena had school in the morning, she knew it was up to her to find the cause so she headed down to the lab about 10:00 p.m. This allowed her to check on Nick and Derrick, and she could spend time testing the specimens in the lab. At this hour, no one would interrupt her. The equipment that she was going to need, namely the gas chromatograph, was not going to be in use. She considered that it may take her most of the night to get the samples examined, but she didn't care. She was determined to find a cause for the deaths and felt she might be getting close.

෧෮

179

Nick didn't want to leave the waiting room as long as Derrick was in critical condition. He had assured Selena that he would be okay, and she knew she could check on him periodically. He got a small cup of hot tea to settle his nerves and took a seat near the lone outside window. As Nick stared at the glass, tears filled his eyes.

"God," he said softly, "why are you letting this happen to me, to Derrick, to the others? I may deserve it, but they don't."

He felt a soft warm arm around his shoulder. Expecting it to be Selena, he turned to see Sandy's tender gaze. "I tried to get back here as soon as I could so that I could be with you. I can't imagine what you're going through."

She hugged him tightly, and Nick couldn't hold back anymore. He sobbed uncontrollably as Sandy tried to console him. Feeling tremendous guilt about how she had treated him at their last encounter, she pressed closer.

"I've been such an ass. I hope you can forgive me," Sandy cried as tears flowed down her cheeks.

"It wasn't your fault. I've been a jerk, and I deserved it. You don't know how much it means to me that you came, because I really need someone with me right now."

"I'll stay as long as you like," Sandy responded, kissing him tenderly on the cheek. "I'm going to try to make up for my mistakes."

His trembling stopped as he looked into her eyes with longing and then placed his arms around her and kissed her tenderly.

CHAPTER 34

Convening the board of directors of Deaconess Hospital in an emergency meeting, Tuttle sullenly addressed those attending.

"Ladies and gentlemen, we have a major problem, as you know from the media reports. Dr Eric Strong, Howard Potwin's partner, will now give us an overview of the medical situation, and then I will outline the emergency plans that we are immediately putting into effect."

Eric reviewed each of the deaths that had occurred in the dialysis facility and pointed out in layman terms the results of the laboratory tests. He brought them up to yesterday's event and then described in greater detail what had happened to Derrick. He went on to explain that in each death the unusual finding of a low anion gap was noted. He further explained that specialized testing was being done on Derrick's blood to try to identify the possible cation or acid that was circulating in these patients' blood. Strong concluded his review and turned it back to Tuttle.

"As you can appreciate, we had to make some drastic changes. We're closing the chronic dialysis facility, and our patients will have their treatments in the hospital dialysis unit where we can give them closer attention until we determine the cause of these deaths."

Eric's cell phone chirped, signaling that he had a message. Selena was texting him. He excused himself and stepped out of the meeting. "What's up?" Eric asked from the hallway.

"I think I found something. The gas chromatography has identified a cation in the serum. It appears to be lithium."

"Lithium? How in the hell would lithium show up in Derrick's blood?"

"I have no idea, but I'm going to test the samples from the other patients to see if lithium was in their blood as well. I can't tell you how in the world it got there, but the test is very accurate."

"This could only suggest that the patients must have been given lithium, because I can't imagine that they were all taking the medication, and it's not used for anything in the dialysis unit."

Visibly shaken, Eric returned to the boardroom and Tuttle.

John Tuttle was just finishing summing up the emergency plans and informing the board about how he intended to deal with the media when Tuttle glanced at Eric. His agitated face said it all. "Is there a problem, Dr. Strong?"

Eric stammered for a moment and then replied, "We may have come across something, but we're double checking the results right now. I hope to be able to give you some answers later today."

After the boardroom cleared, Tuttle pulled Eric aside. "Don't keep me in suspense; what's going on?"

"We don't know for sure. We found lithium in Derrick's blood."

"Lithium, what's that?"

"It's a drug used to treat bipolar illness, a psychiatric disease. It has a very narrow therapeutic range. If you give too little, there's no benefit, but giving too much can be dangerous. It's normally excreted by the kidneys, but with kidney failure, the kidneys would not be able to eliminate the substance, and toxic levels could easily occur."

"So was this boy, Derrick, on lithium?"

"Not that I know of," Eric responded.

"How in the hell would lithium get into the blood, Strong?"

"I have no clue. It's not used in dialysis at all. In fact, it's usually only prescribed by psychiatrists, and if Derrick had been taking this medication, I would have known about it. He seemed to be one of the most upbeat patients we've had on dialysis. He cheered up most everyone he was around."

"So you're saying someone gave this drug to Derrick, right? He wouldn't have access to it himself unless he got it from a pharmacy somehow, correct? If that's the case, is there anyone on the staff who might be angry at you, the hospital, or the patients and would be trying to get revenge?"

"Oh come on, Tuttle. Our dedicated staff would never do anything like that," Eric responded.

"You can't be too careful."

"True, we probably do need to look at personnel records and see if any staff members have a history of bipolar illness or have been treated with lithium."

"For now, let's implement the emergency plan. The nursing director is presently working out a schedule to dialyze the patients in the acute dialysis unit. I'm going to have to call the police department, too. It's certainly beginning to look like foul play was involved."

Although Eric had defended Nancy Campion in the past, Selena had her concerns, and now Tuttle indicated he couldn't trust anyone.

"We have to look at everyone. No one would be exempt from the investigation," Tuttle argued.

⚭

Eric returned to the dialysis unit and feigned ignorance when he found Nancy Campion reviewing Derrick's dialysis run.

"What do you think, Nancy? See any cause for the arrest?"

"No. Not really. Derrick's run was uneventful. In fact, I was just ready to take him off the machine for the night when he coded. Everyone else had gone home, but Derrick had arrived late, so he was the last one to finish."

"What did Derrick look like just before he coded?"

"That's what bothers me. I wasn't right beside his bedside when it happened, but I had gone to get something for Max. I can't even remember what I went to get, but I made sure I had the EpiPen with me. Oh no, Doctor. Now I remember. Max said he had been feeling sick too, and I had gone to get him an emesis basin. What if Max had the same thing happen to him and collapsed on his way home or something!"

"Let's call him now!" Eric said nervously.

The phone rang five times before Max's answering machine picked up. Exasperated, he tried again and with relief, Max answered sleepily.

"Hello, Max?"

"Yeah, what do you want?"

"This is Dr. Strong, and I wondered if everything was okay."

"Yeah, I'm fine. Why are you calling me at home? What time is it?"

"Well, last night I understand you were sick when you came off dialysis, and as you know we've had several patients pass away in the dialysis facility. We were concerned that you may be ill as well. Did you throw up or have any fever or chills?"

"Well, let me think ... no, none of those things. In fact, I felt better after I got out of the unit and had some fresh air. You've never called me at home before. I'm okay, so what's the problem?"

"You were there about the time Derrick arrested on dialysis last night, and since you were sick too, we were all worried that something may have happened to you or that you may be aware of a possible cause. Anything you can add could help us determine what's going on."

"When I left him, he was asleep. Maybe that's from working in that damned pharmacy. Or maybe he's taking drugs. You know he's from the ghetto. You're the hotshot doctor who knows everything. What do you think I could tell you? Too bad Derrick died, such a nice kid and all."

"Oh, Derrick made it; I mean, he's still alive. Did you notice anything unusual going on with him before you left for home?"

"He's still alive?"

"Yes, sir. While I can't discuss his medical condition with you, he's stable at the moment, and we're pursuing diagnostic tests to determine a cause of his arrest."

"So he made it? Where's he at now?"

"He's in the ICU at Deaconess. It was a pretty close call, but it appears that he'll pull through this."

"Well, that's good. What time is it anyway? God! I'm sleepy. Why'd you wake me up at this hour in the morning?"

Eric glanced at his watch and noticed it was 9:00 a.m. "Sorry, Max, I thought you'd be up and didn't want you to be in danger as well. The hospital is going to be moving all the treatments for the patients to the inpatient facility at Deaconess until we get this resolved."

"That so? Well, call back when you don't have to wake me up so damn early," Max replied, slamming down the phone.

Thank goodness the old bastard is all right, even if he is a prick to deal with, Eric thought. *I might try to call Max back at a later time when he's more awake and hopefully in a better mood.*

"Nancy, I wanted to let you know that a substance has shown up in the lab tests. We found lithium in Derrick's blood samples," Eric said, watching for any response from her.

"Really!" Nancy exclaimed, surprised by the report. "Derrick wasn't on lithium, Doctor. I could swear he wasn't."

"I know I didn't prescribe anything like that for him, but it ended up in his bloodstream anyway in what could have been a lethal dose. Once I noticed the anion gap was low, I asked Adam to dialyze him again in the ICU. This morning he is starting to wake up. Did you leave his dialysis machine intact last night?"

"Of course we did. That's standard protocol for anyone who has problems on dialysis. In fact, I'm sure that our biotech sent in the samples of dialysate to be tested already," Nancy responded.

"Good. Actually, the police will likely be showing up later this morning because we're starting to suspect foul play. I'm going to be getting ahold of them today. They'll probably want to talk to you alone and individually with the other personnel as well."

"Police! Am I a suspect?" Nancy asked wearily. She had already surmised that the patients' deaths were caused by someone rather than having been a natural occurrence and was not surprised at Eric's announcement.

"I trust you completely, but the police will have to question everyone, and I thought I would warn you. We don't know how these patients got lithium, but the deaths occurred at the very end of dialysis."

"But I was with Derrick all night, Doctor. I told you on the phone that I had carried an EpiPen in my pocket. When I saw that Derrick had arrested, I quickly injected the epinephrine into his dialysis line. I realized you didn't order this, but I didn't want to see another patient die."

"That was one smart thing to do, Nancy. Not only was it smart, it may have been the very thing that saved Derrick's life."

CHAPTER 35

S elena had completed testing all the saved samples
of serum from the previous victims' blood by six
that morning. She was exhausted but felt a sense of
relief knowing she had found something that the routine lab
evaluations and autopsies had missed. All the samples from
the deceased patients tested positive for lithium. She knew it
was early, but she paged Pam Foster and reported her findings. She then called Professor Buxton's office and left him a
voice mail about the events from yesterday and the finding of
lithium. She thought it was best to return to the ICU waiting
room and check on Derrick and Nick.

Selena found Nick and Sandy together in the ICU waiting
room and thought, *Now this is interesting. Nick certainly
hasn't lost his touch with women; he even attracted a girlfriend in the hospital!*

Smiling, she approached the pair. "Hi, Nick! Is this the
girl you've been telling me about?"

"Selena, I'd like you to meet Sandy Miller," Nick said
warmly.

"Glad to meet you, Sandy," Selena replied, extending her

hand. Then she turned to Nick once more. "What's new with Derrick?"

"The nurses told us he's starting to wake up," Nick replied enthusiastically. "Sandy and I prayed all night for a miracle."

"That's great news," Selena answered. "It'd be horrid for you to lose your best friend. I want you to know that there is some bastard poisoning people. There's a drug called lithium, and it's in Derrick's blood. It's not clear how it got there, but Eric and I are going to find out who and why. That's probably what caused these patients to die, but fortunately, Derrick survived. You probably know, but everyone will be dialyzing here in the hospital where more people can keep an eye on you and the other patients but keep alert."

"Not very reassuring if you ask me," Nick said. "I'm supposed to tackle some guy sticking drugs in my machine at the same time I'm tied down to it. Great!"

"Listen, I'm exhausted," Selena confessed. "I wanted to talk with Pam Foster personally, but I'm going to crash if I don't get some sleep. I'm afraid I'll have to skip my morning classes, but hopefully the professors won't notice. It looks like you two could use some sleep as well."

"You're right, but I don't think I could sleep anyway. I want to stay here with Derrick. The nurses promised me that I could see him in about fifteen minutes, and I'm hoping he'll be alert enough to talk to me.

"Sandy, Selena's right. You should go home and at least get a nap. I'll be just fine. I can't begin to tell you how much it has meant to me to have you here."

Selena followed Nick's eyes as they met Sandy's, and she saw a newfound sincerity in them. Gone were the fraternity playboy and the society jetsetter that she initially knew. Instead, he seemed to be genuine and mature.

"All right, Nick," she replied slowly.

"I'll be back later today," Selena responded, noticing that he seemed oblivious to anything she said.

♋

Leona Ward had not received any notice that the chronic dialysis unit was closed, so when she arrived for her volunteer work, she was surprised to find only a distraught Nancy Campion at her desk in the nurses' station.

"What's going on here?" Leona asked. "This place is deserted!"

"Didn't you hear, Mrs. Ward? Derrick arrested last night, and we had to close the chronic unit until we find out what has happened," Nancy Campion replied.

"Another death? That kid was my son's age!"

"Fortunately, he has survived. He's still in the hospital, and they believe he'll be okay. We're worried that someone might be poisoning the patients."

"Really?" Leona responded with disbelief. "Why would anyone want to hurt one of these unfortunate people?"

"No one knows," Nancy answered with an exhausted expression, bags under her eyes from lack of sleep and worry.

"I've always felt that my decision to donate my son's kidneys was the best decision of my life, and volunteering here has simply confirmed that. Is there anything I can do to help?"

"Leona, keep your eyes and ears open. We don't know who's been doing this, and we can't trust anyone right now. We still haven't been able to contact Derrick's grandmother, who has been raising him, so there's only Nick over at the hospital to visit him now."

"I can go see him if you think they'll let him have visitors. I always felt that Mickey knew I was there even if he was in a coma. Maybe I can help Derrick too. And I'll keep myself alert for anything suspicious. I know how horrid it is to lose a son, and I'll pray for him too. God knows that's the best thing I can offer."

⚭

John Tuttle was reading the newspaper in his office, grumbling about the coverage over the dialysis unit deaths. As usual, his quotes were conveniently adjusted to give the reader the impression that not enough was being done to protect the patients and to raise questions about the safety of dialyzing at the Deaconess Dialysis Facility. As Tuttle scowled at the newspaper, his intercom interrupted his reading.

"Mr. Tuttle, Dr. Strong is here to see you."

"Send him in."

Eric entered Tuttle's office with anticipation of shocking the hospital administrator.

"Well, Doctor, I hope you bring good news for a change. Is there anything to report on this dialysis crisis? I'm tired of hearing bad news."

Eric began, "Mr. Tuttle, we're checking personnel files and looking into every aspect of the drug therapy used in dialysis to try to identify where the lithium came from, but we have a different issue to discuss. I found something in reviewing the tissue typing that is going to be of interest to you."

"Really. Will it get Nick a kidney and get Emilio Seratino off my back?"

Smiling, Eric answered, "It might."

"Let's hear it."

"On reviewing the tissue typing, I went over all of the Seratinos' blood samples. It was curious that Nick didn't match his father's tissue type when Nick should have had half of his father's gene pool but in fact did not, as you recall. This means since his father is a total mismatch, Emilio Seratino is not Nick's father, as we had mentioned before."

"Oh sure, how could I forgot that!" Tuttle responded with astonishment. "So I don't see how that will help Nick, or for that matter help me deal with Emilio Seratino. Should I call him up and tell him, 'Guess what? Nick isn't your child.'"

"No, I don't think that would go over very well." Eric snickered. "But I looked at all the tissue types of patients waiting for transplants, and in doing so I discovered a perfect match for Nick."

"You mean like an identical twin?"

"Not quite. Nick doesn't have a twin out there, but he does have someone he's related to, and that person has his same tissue type. The chance that this person would be unrelated is very slim. You might say one in a million, so this typing suggests the person is genetically connected to him."

"Well, who is it?" Tuttle asked with exasperation, sensing that Strong was dragging the story out to simply antagonize him.

"When typing is performed for our patients, we like to have controls. These are people that are 'off the street,' having no connection to our patients that volunteer to donate blood. Because we don't have people who walk into our transplant office and offer to donate blood, we often use physicians and nurses as volunteers to give blood samples. That's what happened here. Howard Potwin was used as a control, and as it turned out, he is a perfect match for Nick."

"Are you kidding me? So are you saying Howard is related to Nick?"

"Howard appears to be Nick's father. Maybe the transplant program wasn't his only motivation to move Nick up the list. Maybe he wanted his son to get a transplant."

A red-faced John Tuttle looked stunned after fully comprehending what he was being told.

CHAPTER 36

Leona found her way to the ICU. It wasn't easy returning to a place that brought back memories of her son's last hours. Still, she felt a sense of responsibility to help Derrick and his family. She couldn't believe his grandmother wouldn't have arrived by now.

When she stepped into the waiting room, she found a weary Nick and embraced him with a mothering hug. "How's Derrick doing?"

"Better is what the nurses tell me. He recognized me when I saw him last. He squeezed my hand and his eyes met mine. I'm just so glad he survived the poisoning."

"Dear Lord, who do you think might be doing this, and what could possibly be their reason? It just seems hard to imagine that someone would intentionally kill patients already so susceptible."

"I don't know, Mrs. Ward, but I'm keeping my eyes open during my dialysis treatments. No sleeping for me, and quite frankly, I'm scared to death to have those treatments now."

෪

Eric contacted the police department and reached Detective Dave Barrymore. He explained everything that had been happening to the patients. Barrymore had been aware from the reports in the news media, so he wasn't too surprised to get the call.

"So, Detective, we initially thought these patients had died from natural causes, but now with the discovery of lithium in their blood and no other obvious cause of death found on their autopsies, we're concerned they may have been murdered. We believe it's time to have the police investigate. We've done all we can for now. The hospital's CEO, John Tuttle, is aware that you'll be meeting with him."

The detective agreed and immediately drove to Deaconess Hospital. Approaching John Tuttle's secretary with his badge in his hand for identification, he stated, "I believe Mr. Tuttle is expecting me."

"Oh yes. Please go right in," the nervous secretary responded.

Both Eric and John were waiting in the office, and after shaking their hands, Detective Barrymore got right to the point. "So tell me about the deaths that have been occurring."

"The initial deaths were thought to be of natural causes, as I mentioned in the dialysis unit. Dr. Pam Foster, the pathologist who performed the autopsies and her husband, Adam Foster, had been trying to identify a cause." Eric explained everything that had occurred, leading to the suspicions of poisoning by lithium.

"Wouldn't the persons feel this being injected?"

"Actually, they're being dialyzed through a venous and arterial access with IV needles inserted into the vessel, so the patients wouldn't feel anything, although they could see someone do this. If the nurse were giving the drug, the patient would probably assume it was one of the medications they were supposed to receive on dialysis. We've been looking at personnel files to see if any employees have been on lithium or have a history of psychiatric illness where they may be on drugs like lithium. We're also looking at patients' records to see if any are on lithium, but so far none have been found to be on the drug."

"So that is the medication that was used to poison these individuals, right?"

"That's the assumption we're working under, Detective. Fortunately, the last patient survived and is still in our ICU unit."

"Is this patient alert? I'd like to talk with him as soon as possible."

"I believe he's still on a ventilator but is becoming more alert. Adam dialyzed him last night after he got to the ICU, and that probably removed the lithium from his system. Perhaps we can go to his hospital room and try to interview him. He probably won't be able to talk but can write us notes if he is still intubated."

"Also, I need to talk with the head nurse. I understand she was the last person in the dialysis unit when the patient became ill. Do you think she can be trusted?"

"I've told Nancy Campion that you would want to visit with her, but she is one of our best nurses in the hospital, and I can't imagine that she would harm anyone. But we've taken her out of the clinical setting for now, and she's reviewing patients' charts to try and identify any possible cause of the deaths."

"We've got to look at everyone as a potential suspect and not have preconceived opinions about anyone."

"Sure, I understand. Maybe we should first go talk with her. I'll call her now, and we can meet her in dialysis."

GƆ

Nick stood by Derrick's bedside and held his hand, but Derrick couldn't talk because he was still intubated and on the ventilator. Nevertheless, Nick knew that Derrick recognized him. Derrick would squeeze his hand and mouth words.

"Try to relax, Derrick. You're going to be okay. Look who's here. Your grandmother finally made it, and she is so concerned."

"Derrick, Derrick, my baby. What has happened to you? If I had known, I would have been here much sooner. I was visiting your auntie," Priscilla Jones declared.

Nick said, "Mrs. Jones, your grandson seems to be doing better. This is Leona Ward, and she's here to help support you and him. She knows much of what you feel because her son had a serious accident and ultimately donated his kidneys when he passed. I know she can be a great support for you. She has helped all of us in the dialysis center."

The nurse chimed in, affirming what Nick had said. "We hope to have him off the ventilator perhaps later today," the nurse explained. "But Derrick needs some rest now. Perhaps Mrs. Jones could visit with him a few more minutes and the rest of you could return to the waiting room."

Reluctantly, Nick agreed and said goodbye to Derrick but vowed that he would be back at the next opportunity.

GƆ

Eric found Nancy Campion in the dialysis unit with patient charts spread all over her desk and flowcharts laid out to review. He introduced the heavyset man accompanying him to Nancy. She had been warned to expect his visit.

"Nancy, this is Detective Barrymore. He's here to

investigate the dialysis unit deaths and would like to ask you some questions."

Nancy looked up and asked, "Is this a normal conversation, or do I need a lawyer?"

"We're not charging you with anything. We're just investigating a possible crime."

"I couldn't be more upset about their deaths, but some people think I'm responsible, and that makes me nervous."

"We're not jumping to any conclusions. So it is my understanding that you were at the bedside of Derrick Jones before he became ill."

"How did you hear that?"

"Dr. Strong thought you had been by his bedside."

"Well, I was, but I had to get something to help another patient, so I left his bedside momentarily," she responded nervously.

"So was the patient behaving normally before you left him?" the detective asked.

"Yes, as a matter of fact. I don't recall any medical issue going on. He was talking normally, and his last vital signs were unchanged."

"Miss Campion, do you take lithium?"

"No, I don't."

"Do you know if Derrick was on lithium?"

"Not that I recall. Dr. Strong had brought this up to me as well."

"It's our understanding that lithium was found in the blood samples of all the patients who died, as well as in Derrick's blood."

"I'd heard that, but I just can't understand how it would have gotten there."

"That's what we'd like to know. Were any other nurses or family members near the patients when they died?"

"Sure. We have nurses and dialysis techs attending to the patients all the time, but no family members are allowed in the unit when they are dialyzing."

"Do the same nurses or techs take care of the same patients?"

"Yes, for the most part, but obviously there are days when the nurses or techs are off, and then someone else steps in to manage their care."

"Have you looked to see if the same nursing staff were taking care of these patients?"

"There are only twelve patients in the dialysis bay at a time, with one nurse and three techs, so they do all help each other out. I circulate between the bays to help where I'm needed, but basically it would be these four people caring for the patients."

"Who helped you when you tried to resuscitate the patient?"

"Phillip, a nurse, came from the other bay, and everyone still there helped because there were no other patients left. The others had already finished their treatments."

"Have you considered whether any of the staff could have given these patients anything detrimental?"

"Yes, of course I've thought about that, but I can't imagine any of our staff doing anything like that. I must say our nurses and techs are extremely dedicated to our patients and get quite attached to them. We see them three times a week, so when one of them dies, it affects the patients and the staff."

"Was Phillip around the patient before he became ill?

"No, I took care of him myself. I could review their personnel records to see if any of them have had psychiatric issues requiring lithium, but even if they did, which I find doubtful; they wouldn't need to disclose that in their file. I will check Phillip's first."

"What about the other patients?"

"As you probably know, our patients have many medical and psychological issues, so it's possible that one is on lithium. We should have a record of lithium use if we have an accurate list of their medications."

"Why don't you go through those records and see if you find any with such problems."

"Now?"

"Yes, because the sooner we know, the sooner we can exclude this group if it appears none have access to lithium. While you're busy with this, we'll look around at the rest of the dialysis facility. Can you first show me where the patients that died had been sitting for their treatments?"

"Of course. I'll give you a brief tour of the facility and then pull the records to review the charts. Dr. Strong knows the facility very well and can explain much of the area to you. The patients records are electronically recorded, but for the staff we only have personnel files."

CHAPTER 37

Eric led the detective into the water treatment area to begin the tour.

"Detective Barrymore, in this area the water goes through a complex treatment that creates pure water because it is added to the electrolytes that create the dialysate solution. As you can see, it's locked to prevent any outside person from entering or contaminating the area."

Barrymore closely inspected the water and patient treatment areas. "Who can get into this area, Dr. Strong?"

"The biotechnicians, nurses, and dialysis techs, I believe."

"So you're saying any of the dialysis personnel have access."

"That's right. They have to be able to get into this area if there is any problem that would occur to be able to shut off the water treatment if necessary although mostly the biotechnicians work here. If something had been added to the main water supply, however, then all patients would have been affected since it is a central delivery system sending the dialysate to every station."

"That makes sense. So the agent probably was not put into the water here."

"Not likely. It would more apt to have been injected at the bedside."

"Let's see if the nurse has come up with anything," Barrymore concluded.

Returning to Nancy, they found her staring at her computer and going through the files.

"Anything so far?" Eric asked.

"Nothing in the personnel files, and I can't find that any patient is on lithium. At least no one that has lithium listed in his or her charts, but sometimes the patients won't tell us all their medications. There is one interesting finding. Max has a history of bipolar illness but no evidence that he's taking lithium. It does give the names of all his physicians, and Dr. Charles Taylor is listed. Dr. Taylor is a psychiatrist. Maybe we should call his office."

"Absolutely. Nice find, Nancy. Do you have his number?"

"Right here in the medical society handbook. It says he would have office hours now."

Eric dialed.

"Midwest Psychiatry Physicians. Can I help you?

"This is Dr. Eric Strong, and I'm inquiring about one of our patients, Max Strickland."

"Is something wrong with Max?" Lily Jones asked.

"We're not sure. We've been reviewing his list of medications, and although he has listed bipolar illness, it doesn't show that he is on any medical treatment. Has he been getting lithium to treat his illness?"

"Doctor, I'm not sure that I can disclose this to you without the patient's consent. Let me see if Dr. Taylor is available to talk with you. Max doesn't come in often but recently has had some appointments."

The phone line went to hold and a repetitious beeping sound was heard until finally a click and a male voice answered. "Dr. Taylor. Can I help you?"

"Dr. Taylor, this is Dr. Eric Strong from Deaconess Hospital and the dialysis center. One of our patients apparently sees you as well. We are curious if he has been receiving lithium. He has a diagnosis of bipolar disease."

"Max has been in more frequently recently, and I can't really discuss his clinic visits without some permission from him, but I suppose it's important for you to know if he is taking lithium since it is excreted by the kidneys. Funny you should be calling, because Max recently has taken a great interest in his psychiatric health and comes to appointments more often. He insisted that he needed to get back on his lithium after having been off the medication for a long time because he felt he was having more problems with depression combined with manic episodes. He also insisted he was having periods of anger and outrage particularly because of his failure to get a transplant."

Eric's eyebrows rose hearing what was said because everyone had felt Max's wrath over not getting a kidney. Eric knew how difficult Max could be. He often made young nurses get upset and cry.

"He's had his moments in the dialysis unit and in the hospital, but we've become used to dealing with patients like Max. They're often angry and depressed with their disease."

"Well, yes, he has been back on his lithium, and I've been monitoring the levels, but I've been surprised that it has been difficult to get his level into the correct therapeutic range. He seems to be requiring more than I would have ever thought that he would have needed. I've questioned him if he was taking the drug as prescribed, and he insists that he hasn't missed a dose."

"Thank you, Dr. Taylor, that is very helpful. We'll get back with you if we need more information."

Hanging up, Eric paused for a moment, running through

his mind whether Max could be a killer. Even though Max could be difficult, he still found it hard to believe Max would do such a thing.

His quietness was apparent to Barrymore, who saw that he was visibly shaken. "Is something wrong?"

"Dr. Taylor just confirmed that Max was prescribed lithium recently, but he also mentioned that although Max has been getting his prescription filled, the levels are inadequate. He's questioned him whether he had been taking the medication and he has insisted that he hasn't missed a dose."

"Where's Max's position in the unit compared to the other patients?"

"I'll show you, but he has been right next to the patients who have passed. You see, when one patient died, we shifted the others and they either sat to his right or his left."

"Have you talked to Max lately?"

"I talked with Max after Derrick's cardiac arrest to ensure he was okay, since he was sitting next to Derrick and had left dialysis shortly before Derrick became ill. He was reportedly not feeling well that day before he left, but he seemed upset that I even bothered him. He was the last person in the dialysis unit except for Derrick."

"Let's call him now and see if he's home. If he is, we'll go there now to question him."

The phone rang multiple times but no one answered. Eventually a gravelly voice answered on the voice recording, "I'm not home. If you're calling to sell something, hang up. I don't want it. If this is something important, then leave a message. Otherwise, goodbye—I don't want to hear from you."

That's Max, Eric thought.

"This isn't good," the detective said. "I think we need to get to the hospital. If he isn't home, he may be going to the hospital to see the one patient that survived in order to finish the job."

ᘜᘝ

Damn! The kid lived! Max Strickland thought. He replayed the previous evening's events, and it occurred to him that Derrick might have not been fully asleep when he had added the lithium to the dialysate solution.

What if Derrick had seen him by the machine?

He felt confident that Nancy Campion had fallen for his act of being sick. It appeared to have distracted her long enough to allow the lithium to have its full effect without her noticing anything unusual. But Derrick should have died! And having him live was allowing a potential witness to identify him as a killer. He decided there needed to be another 'unfortunate incident' that would happen to Derrick in the hospital. He began plotting out an alternative plan. This time he couldn't afford to miss, so Max Strickland took a saucer from his kitchen cabinet and began to crush lithium tablets into a fine powder.

Let's see, now how many tablets will I need to get the job done? I think maybe ten will do it, but to be on the safe side, I think I'll crush fifteen. After all, the kid survived that the last hit I gave.

Max poured the powder in a test tube with hydrochloric acid to create lithium chloride. He had read online that lithium chloride would be soluble and create a liquid state. He poured the liquid into a test tube and put a cork on the end, placing the tube in his pocket. He pulled out a syringe and needle from his kitchen drawer that he had stolen from the dialysis unit and added this to his pocket. Grabbing his car keys, he began mapping out his strategy to get to Derrick.

On arriving at Deaconess Hospital, he went to the information center and asked where Derrick was located. "My good friend from dialysis, Derrick Jones, was admitted recently, and I would really like to visit him and encourage him. Can you give me his room number?"

"Mr. Jones is located in MICU, bed three. Are you immediate family?"

"No, just a very good friend."

"I'm not certain that you'll be able to get into the ICU. Normally only family are allowed."

"Oh, but it's so important that I see him. I know that I can give him encouragement to get better."

"I would suggest that you try the intercom at the entrance to the ICU and see if the nurse will allow you to visit."

"Thank you." Max smiled as he mumbled "damn." Making his way to the ICU, he tried the intercom and the voice answered, "Can I help you?" Max gave his story about the importance of seeing Derrick, but the ICU nurse didn't budge. "I'm sorry, but you would need to come in with family to visit him."

Drat, Max thought. *There's got to be another way into this place*

Max stood in the hall, watching the medical personnel coming and going. He noticed that most did not go through the main entrance to the ICU but rather a back entrance after using their badge to unlock the door. Carefully, he stood by the entrance as people went in or out, looking for an opportunity to go in.

He finally saw his chance as one of the Hispanic cleaning ladies who barely spoke English opened the door and pushed her cart into the ICU. He carefully followed her in, making sure he stayed behind the cart that helped hide him from being seen.

Barrymore and Eric hurried across the street, making their way to the hospital entrance. Eric was trying to decide the best way to get to the ICU. They stopped at the information desk to question whether anyone had asked about Derrick.

"Yes, there was an elderly gentleman who said he was Derrick's best friend and that he had to see him to give him encouragement. I told him that only family would be allowed in, but I did give him the room number in the MICU."

"About how long ago was that?"

"Only about ten minutes ago."

"Detective, I think that we should take the stairs. The elevators can be slow, and I sense we need to get to Derrick's bedside now."

"I'm fine with that."

They quickly climbed the back stairwell up four flights. Barrymore was breathing heavily from his excess weight, but Eric was used to running the stairs and had stayed in shape.

They ran into Adam and Pam Foster, and Eric quickly explained. "It's Max. We need to get to Derrick's room."

"What?"

"No time to explain. We need to get there now."

Running down the halls, the four made their way to the ICU. They used Eric's badge to enter the back door. Racing to room three, they found Max standing by Derrick. In his hand was a syringe. Derrick was awake but couldn't talk because of the endotracheal tube in place, but his eyes told everything. They were wide open and filled with fear as he saw Max look for a place to inject the lithium into a port of his IV.

"Max, stop right there. It's over!" Eric yelled.

The detective grabbed Max's arm, restraining him from injecting the solution. The commotion attracted the ICU nurses to room three, and soon a crowd surrounded the room and Derrick's bedside. Max's hands were pulled behind his back and the detective used a zip tie to secure them. He radioed for backup, and sirens could be heard in the distance. Max was led out of the ICU with onlookers wondering just what was going on.

It didn't take the press long to hear of the news, and reporters were soon at the hospital wanting the latest information.

John Tuttle mulled over what he was going to say and told the hospital receptionist to send them to his conference room so he could talk with them there.

After cameramen and reporters were all gathered together and with cameras rolling and microphones assembled, John Tuttle spoke slowly, with Eric by his side. "Today we have discovered the cause of the deaths of these unfortunate dialysis patients. Dr. Strong will give you the details and what has transpired."

"We believe one of our dialysis patients became disgruntled about his failure to receive a kidney transplant. He was apprehended and is now in custody. We should know more in the next few days, but that's all we know at this time."

A myriad of questions were fired at Eric and Tuttle, asking for names and more circumstances, but they refused to address questions. Leaving the room, both men looked weary. Tuttle contemplated how terrible this was for the hospital and the dialysis patients. It also occurred to him that although Emilio Seratino wasn't killing patients to get his son a kidney, he was trying to subvert the system for his son. He began to realize how desperate these patients and their families can become because the number of kidneys available for transplantation were so limited.

Eric was right, he thought. *We can't make exceptions and give priorities to a few. These people are desperate and deserve to be treated equally.*

Although not condoning the actions of these people, he wondered if he would have considered doing something similar if he or his child were in the same circumstance, but he knew it wouldn't justify bending the rules, or for that matter killing people.

I still have to deal with Potwin. What the hell is up with that?

CHAPTER 39

With all the events of the previous day behind him, Eric thought it was time to address the issue of Howard Potwin being Nick's father. He went directly to Tuttle's office to finally put this to rest. The receptionist had seen him a lot lately so she didn't hesitate to let him go right in. Everyone knew of the events from yesterday and Max's arrest.

"John, we need to have Howard come in so we can discuss this paternity issue."

"I agree, Eric. I'm not sure what I'm more shocked about, Max or Howard."

Calling his secretary on the intercom, he asked her to page Dr. Potwin to come to his office for a meeting. Potwin always returned Tuttle's pages quickly, and this was no exception.

He was escorted to the conference room where the door was closed. Eric, with a somber face, was sitting at the conference table waiting for his arrival. Before closing the door, Tuttle asked his secretary to be sure they were not disturbed.

"So, Howard, there's been a discovery in the tissue typing

of the Seratino boy that needs an explanation from you. Eric, can you give us the summary of your findings?" Tuttle asked.

Eric began slowly and cautiously, knowing Potwin was his boss and the senior physician. "Adam and I were reviewing the tissue typing results of our current patients when we were trying to find a link with the deaths of the patients. As you know, we found that each patient who died was high up on the transplant list. This led to the possibility they were being killed to remove them from the list, but in the process of reviewing the tissue typing we discovered a match for Nick Seratino. That match was you, Howard."

Potwin's face turned red as he looked downward with embarrassment. "I, I do have an explanation. Nineteen years ago, when I was going through a divorce, I attended a fundraising event for Deaconess, and you probably know of my love for opera. At this gala was an opera singer with a magnificent voice. That singer was Rosa Seratino, and I became infatuated with her. We ended up together for the night, but she warned me never to contact her because her husband could be ruthless. I later discovered that he had mafia ties and would get what he wanted one way or another.

"When Nick became your patient with renal failure, I didn't know what to do. I tried to talk to Rosa and she basically wanted me to do anything I could to help him. When her husband offered to make the large contribution, I thought this opened the door to get Nick the kidney. I know I should have told you, but I wasn't sure I really was the father."

"From the looks of the tests, you are the father, Howard," Eric Strong reiterated.

"What do we do now?" Tuttle asked.

"I don't think there's any value in telling Emilio Seratino," Eric responded. "That would simply create more problems, but I think I have an idea. Howard, would you consider donating your kidney to Nick? You know we're doing more living non-related kidney transplants than ever before, and Emilio doesn't have to know you're related. We can simply say you're sympathetic to this young man and want to help the transplant program. It should give him an excellent outcome with the great match that you have with him. What do you think?"

"Well, I'm in good health, and I think it's the least I can do for a son I've never been able to claim. I actually have become rather fond of the young man. He has really matured with this illness, and I'm proud of him."

Eric said, "John, should we talk to Seratino together. If so, I can set up a meeting in our office. It'll be interesting to see his wife's reaction when we tell them Howard's going to donate a kidney."

"Give them a call, and we'll meet with them tomorrow. I think the sooner we get this behind us the better."

The following day the Seratinos were escorted to Eric Strong's office. Adam Foster, Eric Strong, Howard Potwin, and John Tuttle were seated around the large conference table.

Eric greeted them first. "Emilio, Rosa, thank you so much for coming. We think we have good news for Nick. We've been reviewing our tissue typing and discovered a match for your son that will work for a successful transplant. Howard here has been found to be a great match for your son, and because of his concern about Nick and our transplant program, he'd like to volunteer to be the donor."

Emilio's eyes opened wide and he nearly shouted, "Well, by God, it's about time. We've been so concerned that Nick wouldn't survive everything that has been going on in the dialysis unit."

"Are you still willing to support our program with your

donation? This will really help many of our patients who can't afford their medications, or for that matter the evaluation needed to get a kidney transplant."

"Of course I will. My word is my word. When can we get this going?"

"Howard here will need to undergo some tests to make sure that he has no contraindication to donating a kidney, but we don't anticipate there should be any problem. I would say if we expedite the testing, we can get the transplant within the month," Eric responded.

"Perfect. That's good news isn't it, Rosa?"

Rosa smiled as she glanced at Howard Potwin. "Very good news. I'm so thankful to Dr. Potwin."

CHAPTER 40

Max Strickland was booked into the county jail. His rights had been read, and after initially stating he would defend himself, he later decided he needed outside counsel. His dialysis treatment was due the following day, so Adam Foster was trying to decide how they could provide his treatments in the facility where he had killed some of the patients. It was decided they would dialyze him in the isolation area removed from the general unit, and the guard could be posted outside the room.

Eric called the police department and talked with Detective Barrymore. "Detective, we're working on the logistics to dialyze Max. We'll need to have guards outside the room where he will be running. That shouldn't be a problem, right?"

"No, we do that all the time. If he's found guilty, he'll have a sentence of life imprisonment and would be transferred to a state prison. They have their own dialysis facility."

"You know I shouldn't feel sorry for Max, but I realize the desperation of our patients. The Seratinos were exploring every option, including buying kidneys overseas, putting pressure on family and friends to donate, and bribing our transplant program. We have many patients that survive on dialysis, but it's very difficult for them. What do think will happen to Max?"

"He'll most likely be found guilty. The courts will probably be sympathetic and give him a long sentence, as I mentioned, but he'll be able to live out his life similar to what he was having out of prison. He may get released early with good behavior, but I doubt he'll ever get a transplant, which was his goal even though sinister means."

"In some strange way, I hope it works out for him."

The workup for Howard Potwin was expedited to ensure that his renal function was normal, that he had no underlying illnesses that would compromise his remaining renal function in the future, and that he was healthy enough to donate a kidney. Howard was right. He was in good health, and the testing proved it.

The transplant for Nick was set up for the following week and was to take place on Tuesday. After the transplant team reviewed Nick's medical records, they could find nothing that would prohibit him receiving the transplant.

The day of surgery came quickly, and Nick nervously arrived at the admission office of Deaconess with his parents and Sandy.

"I'm Nick Seratino, and I'm here to receive a kidney transplant," Nick stated to the receptionist.

"How exciting!" the clerk exclaimed. "Are you getting a transplant from a family member?"

"No, actually, just an acquaintance of the family."

"How generous they must be."

Sandy Miller chimed in. "We're so grateful to Dr. Potwin that he agreed to donate a kidney."

"Wow, you must be special to have one of our own be your donor. He is a very respected physician on our staff."

Nick helped getting on the wristband that identified him as a patient and was taken to room 7046 on the renal floor where the nurses began taking his vital signs and reviewing his medications. The room seemed eerily familiar since this was the floor where it all began in the first place with renal failure.

Adam Foster's cell phone began buzzing, alerting him to a page from Eric Strong. "Eric, what's happening?"

"Good news, Adam. You know that kidney donor that we had last night from the car accident?"

"Yeah, sure. Any of our patients getting one of the kidneys?"

"Yes, Derrick Jones is almost a perfect match!"

"Incredible! Derrick is off the ventilator and was up in the chair today. He has had nothing by mouth, so I don't see any reason why we can't go ahead with the transplant. He's been great otherwise and should be a good candidate. He's right here, and I have no doubt that he will consent to go ahead. I've always wanted this kid to get a break."

"Nick Seratino just checked into the hospital, so I'm going to arrange for them to be in the same room to start out. Afterward, they'll need to be separated in their own private rooms, but I know they'll be excited to be together now."

Eric made his way to the seventh floor and walked into Nick's room to perform the physical exam. "Nick, are you all ready for today?"

"Quite frankly, I'm nervous. You know I really didn't have any medical problems prior to this kidney thing, and now I get poked and jabbed all the time. I've never been put under for a procedure until this illness but I couldn't be more excited to get the gas now for the transplant."

"Well, just start counting to ten, and before you get to five you'll be asleep. You won't feel anything. But I have some news for you. You're going to have a special roommate today. Derrick Jones is getting a transplant today too. I've asked that the two of you start out together in this room. He'll be transferring here in just a few minutes. The transplant coordinator talked to him and he is on his way. He is totally over the lithium overdose, so we didn't see any reason that we couldn't proceed."

"Wow, I am so happy for him! He deserves the kidney more than I do. He's been waiting a long time and is such a great guy. It will be good for us to be together, but I just hope both our new kidneys work."

"They should, barring an unforeseen problem. You both have the perfect match."

When Derrick arrived at Nick's room, Nick lost it. Tears streamed down his face from all the emotion he was feeling. "Derrick, I'm so happy you're alive and now getting a transplant the same time that I am."

He hugged Derrick, and Derrick hugged him back.

Derrick said, "Hey, man, we're in this together. Can't get better than this."

Emilio arrived just as Derrick was settling into his room. "Son, big day today. We get to start over."

"So does Derrick." Nick pointed to his roommate.

"How about that? I'd say we have a miracle happening. You boys are going to be blood brothers—sorry, I mean kidney brothers!"

That seemed to calm Nick's nerves as he changed into the not-so-covering hospital gown. "These gowns aren't exactly the most stylish, are they?"

"Not really," Derrick responded. "But we can show off our pecs and biceps."

"Yeah, right. Probably mostly just glutes instead. Well, the problem is they've all faded since I started on this journey."

"They'll come back, I'm sure."

Derrick was taken first to the operating room where the anesthesiologist prepared to administer the IV sedation for the surgery. The IV line had already been established to provide access for the intravenous sedation. Within minutes, Derrick was asleep, and the harvested kidney was brought to the operating room in a cooler. Eric made the incision in the groin area where he would insert the kidney. He dissected down to the fascia and the iliac artery. Once he identified the iliac vein and the ureter, the harvested kidney was attached to the artery and vein, and Derrick's ureter was attached to the ureter of the new kidney. Immediately after the blood supply was established to the kidney, it turned pink. Within minutes, urine began to flow into the bladder, and Eric Strong smiled beneath his mask, for he never grew tired of watching this miracle occur. Derrick was transferred to the surgical ICU for close observation overnight. Since large amount of IV fluids were administered during the operation, Derrick's face was quite swollen, but his urine output was magnificent, and he began to lose the swelling that had accumulated during his surgery.

Nick Seratino went through the same scenario, but in this case, Howard Potwin was taken to an adjoining room. His kidney was removed through small incisions using a laparoscope. It was then transferred immediately to the next operating room, where Eric Strong skillfully inserted Potwin's kidney into Nick Seratino. Again there was immediate urine output, and Potwin's transplanted kidney was pink and healthy appearing once blood supply was established to the kidney. Nick was subsequently transferred to the ICU next to Derrick, where both spent the night under careful observation. By morning they were awake and already taking small walks down the hall.

"Wow, Derrick can you believe it? We can pee!" Nick cried, giving him a thumb's-up.

"Not exactly. It's going into this bag. Not quite the same. I would rather shoot it against the wall."

"I doubt the nurse would like that."

"Yeah, but wouldn't it feel good?"

"You're right, but we're making urine again. I'm just glad of that, and the pain isn't that bad from the surgery."

"I would take this pain any day."

"Me too, brother. I can't believe this happened to both us at the same time. They're transferring me out today. How about you?"

"I think so. They tell me our rooms will be right next to each other."

"Yeah, that's what I understand as well. No problem from my standpoint, 'cause I'll just walk next door."

The laboratory values were checked daily and sometimes twice a day. The drug levels of the antirejection drugs were also tested and the drugs adjusted accordingly. After four days in the hospital, both young men were dismissed, but they were told they would need to have lab testing three times a week.

"I guess this poking and prodding doesn't stop yet, does it, Derrick?" Nick said.

"You're right, but it'll be okay. I guess I am sort of getting used to it," Derrick responded.

"I'm not sure I ever will. I just hate needles," Nick said.

CHAPTER 41

"Wow, I think I can be more sympathetic to my patients. The pain from this surgery isn't great, but I can live with it," Howard Potwin exclaimed.

He knew going into the peritoneal cavity causes a slowing of the bowel function, so he was on clear liquids for the first day. Using a laparoscopic technique, however, did speed up the healing process, and by day six he was well enough to go home. His creatinine was checked and was 1.5mg%—not bad for a guy with only one kidney. He knew it might get better with time.

As he was wheeled to the exit of the hospital, he contemplated all that had happened. *I can't believe I just gave a kidney to my son, and I helped our transplant program with the large donation from Emilio Seratino.*

It felt good being a perfect match.

Eric Strong was riding high after a week with two successful transplants. He wasn't on call for the weekend, and he couldn't wait to take Selena to dinner. He knew she had been very stressed over the deaths in the dialysis unit and from blaming herself for not recognizing Nick's illness and for that matter suspecting Nancy Campion as the murderer when Nancy actually had saved Derrick's life. He felt with the transplant completed and appearing to be a success, she would be feeling much better. He called Adam and Pam to join them for dinner to celebrate. With everything that had happened, this called for a special night. He drove his 911 Porsche Cabriolet, and it was surprisingly warm enough to put the top down. He loved feeling the air whipping past his face.

Texting Selena, he gave her a head's up that he had arrived. *Ready to go, sweetheart?*

I'll be right down, came the text back.

The striking strapless dress drew attention to her perfectly sculpted figure.

Eric's eyes widened and appeared to glaze over as he proceeded to study her figure from top to bottom. "You look stunning tonight. Are you sure you want to go out to dinner with me?"

"No one that I would rather be with tonight."

The wind whipped through Selena's hair as he drove. They arrived at Antonio's Restaurant and turned the car over to the valet. He had arranged for a special table that was sequestered in the back of the restaurant, for he knew the owner and had cared for some of his family members. Adam and Pam had already arrived and had ordered Dom Perignon for the occasion.

Antonio watched them come in and immediately went to greet them. "Who is this great-looking couple?" he exclaimed. "We need to give them only the best table in the house. They must be movie stars."

Selena blushed as she noticed how his eyes checked out her seductive gown. "Not a movie star, just a graduate student, but I'm still very happy to be eating at your restaurant."

The wonderful smells of tomato, garlic, oregano, basil, and other spices permeated the air, reminding Selena of her family's cooking.

"I'll try to live up to your expectations, because we have prepared a special dinner for the four of you."

Toward the back of the restaurant in a secluded location was the table for the four. The bottle of Dom Perignon was placed in an ice bucket, ready to be popped open. There was a faint scent of lavender from the fresh flowers on the table, but Selena's Marc Jacobs perfume, Daisy Dream, was what Eric noticed the most. Like a true gentleman, he held the chair out for her. Their eyes met as the four toasted with the champagne. Selena's clear olive complexion was glowing from the candle on the table, her hair draped sensuously over her shoulders, her dark eyes peering deeply into Eric's.

Adam stopped them for a moment—"Ahem, we're over here. Remember, we came tonight too"—realizing that Eric and Selena were in a world of their own.

"Sorry. I guess I was a little focused on Selena."

"And you should be. Let's test this champagne."

The waiter poured each another glass of champagne, and they toasted several times, gratified that everything turned out well for Nick and Derrick—sad that they had three patients die yet thankful they were able to stop Max before more were killed.

The moment was interrupted when the waiter brought an antipasto, which included bruschetta, figs, eggplant in a tomato puree, sliced Italian-style meats, olives, and assorted breads served with a pinot grigio, for them to begin their dinner. The main entrée of veal and lemon saltimbocca made with prosciutto, lemon, white wine, tomatoes, sage, and cream and served with a 1995 Banfi Brunello di Montalcino followed.

As they slowly ate, Eric and Selena reminisced about how they met and fell in love and the irony of Nick's illness in the midst of their courtship. They reflected on the deaths of the patients and how the drive to find the cause brought them closer together. Now that Nick had a kidney and Max was arrested, their lives could resume a more normal path.

"So, Eric, I believe my father thinks you're the greatest since Nick is doing so well. You know Nick has always been the favorite in the family. It's kind of an Italian thing with the son in the family, but I do think he is respecting me more now that I discovered the cause of death of the patients."

"He should respect you. You're intelligent, beautiful, and hardworking. Your father could have no better daughter than you. He must be extremely proud of you."

"Well, I hope so, but like I said, the boys in the family seem to take precedence."

As the four finished their main meal, Eric feigned dropping his spoon on the floor and knelt down to pick it up. Reaching into his pocket, he pulled out a small wooden box and gazed into Selena's eyes again but with a twinkle in his.

Opening the box a small LED light showered a beam onto a three-carat diamond, projecting a mass of crystal sparkles in all directions.

Selena looked down at him and began to cry. She valued her ability to always maintain control of her emotions, but this one time it wasn't possible.

Eric smiled as he said, "Will you marry me? I want to spend the rest of my life with the most beautiful girl in the world."

Through tears of joy, Selena blurted out, "Yes, yes! Of course, yes!"

Adam and Pam had been cued in that this was going to happen and immediately congratulated the couple.

Antonio also knew what Eric had planned, so he was prepared with a camera to record the special event. He snapped picture after picture. And turning to the sous chef watching with him, he said, "What a beautiful thing. I'm so glad we could be part of this evening because they are the perfect match."

Shortly after that special moment, Emilio and Rosa entered the restaurant to see the newly engaged couple. Emilio had a huge smile as he approached them. Eric had given them the time to come when he had asked for Selena's hand in marriage. Emilio, Rosa, Selena, and Eric all embraced, and Antonio brought more champagne to toast their engagement.

"Selena, I want you to know that I am so proud of your intelligence, especially in attracting a smart, good-looking man. We're going to have movie-star grandchildren," Emilio responded.

"Oh, Emilio, don't put them in such an awkward position. Those children will come in due time," Rosa said.

"Listen, we've had a perfect kidney match for our son, and now the perfect man for our daughter. I can't think of anything better—well, except for perfect grandchildren. We must have done something right."

With that, Rosa gave a smile, knowing there was more to the story.

But he would never know.

AUTHOR'S NOTE

There are 468,000 people on dialysis in the United States, 193,000 who have had a kidney transplant, with 93,000 people waiting for one, according to the US Renal Data System Annual Data Report, 2018. Having kidney failure and surviving on dialysis is not easy. In *The Perfect Match,* I hope the reader will appreciate the difficulties and challenges facing people with kidney failure. In addition, I hope the reader recognizes the generosity of those who donate their kidney or that of a loved one who passes away. It is truly the gift of life. A portion of the proceeds of this book will be donated to the Fresenius Kidney Foundation.